The Boddicker Letters

By A.C. Cross

The Boddicker Letters

Copyright © 2023 Aaron C. Cross

Acknowledgements

To my mother and brother as we move through life differently now.

To my cover artist Luke Tarzian for the beautiful artwork and layout.

To my fantastic beta readers Rory August and Steve Westenra for giving me new, generous, and needed insight on the book.

To my author, blogger, and editor friends for giving me a community to work within.

To my readers for giving me a chance to do what I love.

To everyone with stories waiting to come out of you.

To all of you,

Thank you from the bottom of my heart. Please enjoy.

From the desk of the Editor:

Forgive me, reader, for I am cognizant of the utter madness which lurks in the pages to come. What I am duty-bound – honor-bound – to show you henceforth shall not make sense to you. Nor should it. I myself can scarcely comprehend the words sent to me. Yet, I have been tasked with a solemn responsibility to compile, transcribe, and submit to the general populace the words and stories therein submitted to his love by Mr. Titus Boddicker.

I shall explain further 'fore continuing. My name is Solomon Trench and my profession is that of Editor-in-Chief for the Poughkeepsie Tribune in this, the year of our Lord nineteen-hundred and twenty-two. In my position at the Tribune, I have been intimately acquainted with all manner of curiosities and befuddlements that the world may place in front of us. I have interviewed dictators and mass murderers. I have spent time in war-torn countries and exposed an epidemic of opium misuse. I have taken great pride in my evenhanded portrayal of even the vilest of humanity, for I believe the word of the press is sacrosanct and must be treated with due respect and humility. A lie, once printed, becomes inscribed as truth and damns the rest of us.

All this, my friends, is to say that I have not once considered altering the contents of these letters. Despite the increasing concern I had for the author and his life when reading through them, I feel as if it is necessary to present to you all the facts as they were given to me. You may find them foolish or absurd. A likelihood, in fact, that. Yet, I believe in nothing more than the veracity and integrity of the written word, especially from one as esteemed as Mr. Boddicker.

You will notice points where the text becomes indecipherable or messy. Handwritten typos, as it were. I assure you, reader, that I have transcribed everything exactly as I saw it. Some pages were damp. Some burned and charred. Some had drawings or scribbles on them that signified something or another. I am no scholar. I cannot tell you what those drawings are, nor may I replicate them here. However, I have done my best to describe them as best I can to provide you the depth of the madness which lurks in the letters.

Dear reader, please do not judge harshly any of us involved in this enterprise. We know not what we do and I am certain that Mr. Boddicker did not either.

For now, I am your humble transcriptionist.

Solomon Trench

Editor-in-Chief, Poughkeepsie Tribune

December 23, 1921

My darling Luisa,

My love and light. I know that you are confused, perhaps hurt, by my sending you away to your parents for the holiday season, but I beg you to read this letter so that I may explain myself further.

I should have thought that the universe, in its infinite wisdom, would have seen fit to place me in a profession suited to my intellect and talents. A doctor, perhaps, or a lawyer. A politician, maybe! Imagine that! Me, your Titus, a politician. The idea is ludicrous, but I digress. However much I would have expected from life, the tragic comedy of existence has reduced me to the position of a mere solicitor. I chafe every day at the unfairness of the life set before me and under the yoke placed upon me by the odious forces that employ me. I do not hate the men specifically. As humans, they are fine enough. We speak and exchange tales of our lives during our luncheons. However, it is the role they play in my life that I cannot abide. They pay me a pittance to debase myself in such a thankless, anonymous role. Is my dignity worth so little? Apparently so, at least according to the penny-pinching misers that own and operate this place of business, though I scarcely may say it warrants such a lofty title. I would rather send the fleas to do my work than continue another day.

My feelings about the life placed in front of me, however, are not unknown to you. Though I have endeavored to mask my hostility from you with as much love and adoration as I am capable of providing, you are too wise to not see the discontent that lurks within my breast. You have spoken to me softly, encouragingly. You have dried my tears and wiped the sweat from my brow as I return home. You keep the hearth of your love warm to melt the ice around my heart. You have saved me from an early grave, dear Luisa, and the extent of my gratitude should not be surpassed were the Lord to bring upon another great Flood to wash away the sins of the world. I am indebted to you with my very soul.

It brings me some joy then, my darling, to inform you of the purpose of sending you to your parents for Christmas. My reasoning is such: I shall not be present! Indeed, come Christmas morning, I shall board a train to a small town across the state to set off on a true adventure. One that could assure our future together will be prosperous and as plentiful as you and I deserve.

I can hear your voice now, the dulcet tones soft and gentle, asking me what could have possessed me to leave you behind in such a time as this. My angel, I have been employed in such a capacity as I deserve! Not more than a week prior to this letter, I was approached on my walk home by an elderly couple who asked for a few moments of my time. Though I wished nothing more than to come home to you, I acquiesced. They seemed to be in a state of distress and, though my position as a solicitor may imply otherwise, I am still a gentleman through to my bones. It behooved me to stop and aid them, as you would have insisted I do as well.

They introduced themselves as Mr. Leland and Mrs. Miriam Weatherby and I recognized the names, as I'm sure you do too! The Weatherbys have been one of the city's leading families for decades, though they have been quiet as of late. Indeed, I did not identify them at first, as their clothes were uncharacteristically shabby and they appeared disheveled. Exhausted. Fearful. Haunted, one may say. Upon seeing them in that state, I quickly ushered them to a nearby cafe so we could speak privately and provide them some nourishment. As we ate, they explained the reason behind their distress.

A month ago, they told me, their son Lucien received a message from a Mr. Marsh, inquiring about his availability as a schoolteacher for the upcoming semester. As they said, Lucien was ecstatic, as he had become withdrawn and despondent after being fired from his previous position as a teacher in Boston. They would not go into detail about the circumstances of his removal from such a position, but they assured me that it was for nothing prurient or untoward. In their words, he simply was unable to acclimate to the requirements of living in such a large town. However, this new position would have meant a significant increase in his pay from the previous position and he was told specifically in the letter that he would find a permanent home were he to choose to accept the offer. Sight unseen, he decided to pack up his things and travel to the town to accept the offer in person. Foolish, perhaps, but we were all young and headstrong once, weren't we, my love? You still remain young as I get older and older by the year, a tribute to the beauty that God has bestowed upon you.

As they explained about the position, I could see pride in their eyes at the success of their progeny. However, when they turned to the subject of the conversation at large, the glitter in their eyes disappeared, replaced by a weariness that startled me. They told me that Lucien had made a phone call home every night for the first week of his tenure, speaking excitedly about the town and his home and the school. He waxed poetic about how quaint the location was and how the locals, though initially skeptical of him, soon warmed to him and included them among their events and poker nights. He promised that he would not fall prey to gambling and loose women and that he would be home as soon as he could manage.

After that final conversation, though, they had not heard from him since. They had telephoned and asked for him, but received angry responses in return, excoriating them for interfering with the town's business and their son's life. They were called all sorts of names of various vulgarities and were hung up on. Naturally, they were furious and sent the police to investigate. However, only a day or two later, the police returned and informed them that there was no sign that Lucien had ever arrived in the town and that the police were unwilling to invest more time in such a wild goose chase while actual crimes were being committed. The police left and desperation sank in for the Weatherbys. They tried to enlist the services of others but were rebuffed at every turn. Mr. Weatherby himself tried to charter a boat to take him to the town, but found none willing to take him.

It was at this point that I began to worry about what they were to ask. If the police were unwilling to aid them, what could a simple solicitor do for them? I asked them and they assured me that they needed my help and experience. Before I could further enquire as to what experience they referred to, Mr. Weatherby retrieved a chunk of gold the size of a woman's fist from the pocket of his overcoat and set it on the table. He told me that, before Lucien disappeared, he had told them that he was being paid with gold rather than paper money and wanted to verify that it was, in fact, pure. They had received a few samples and taken them in to be appraised. They had been informed that the gold was indeed pure and of finer quality than the jeweler had ever seen. The value, Mrs. Weatherby told me, was estimated at around twenty-thousand dollars and that every single ounce they had received from Lucien was mine if I accepted the task of traveling to the town and retrieving their son from whatever nasty business he had clearly become enmeshed in.

Though further questions would have been prudent, the glint of the gold so blinded me that I agreed wholeheartedly and told them that I would be off as soon as I could possibly manage. The relief on their faces was palpable and, for a moment, I felt guilty at taking their money. However, my love, I see this as a boon! This windfall will provide me the ability to find another job more suited to my abilities and temperament. I shall be happier and more fulfilled and, in turn, should likely be able to provide you the children you have asked of me for years now. My darling, we shall both benefit from a simple excursion. I promised nothing to them so, should I not find their son, I would hardly be culpable of malfeasance.

All of this is to say, darling Luisa, that I am aggrieved to not be with you during the holidays, but the long-term future of our family depends on such a minor inconvenience. Please, enjoy your time with your parents. Eat well and celebrate the birth of our Lord! I shall be traveling on Christmas morning to Innsmouth, Massachusetts, though I hope to return to you and our home no later than the New Year.

I miss you already and it feels as if my heart is gone.

I love you beyond words.

You are my light and my wind.

Take care, my dove.

Your beloved Titus

December 25th, 1921

My beautiful Luisa,

Happy Christmas, angel! I am *finally* sitting in my hotel room in Innsmouth as I write to you now. Darling, I hope that your Christmas was peaceful and comforting, as mine has been neither. Please, regale me with tales of your holiday with your relatives! Did you have the roast duck this year as usual, or did the old man wish for something different? A ham, perhaps? And your nieces and nephews? Were they holy terrors, save sweet Annella who is always so gentle? I apologize for the questions, love. I merely ask because I already wish to be home and with you, though I have only just arrived in this place.

My love, to say that my travel here was difficult would be to understate the experience. I have never in my life endured such a frustrating, uncomfortable journey. My original plan of taking the train was damaged when the engine somehow broke beyond repair. All taxicabs were booked or unavailable. I certainly was not going to *walk* the hours required. Finally, I managed to secure passage on a ship bound for Innsmouth, though the vessel only managed to stay above water through God's grace.

You see, nearly as soon as the ship set off, we were inundated with rain and sleet and all manner of troublesome weather. Now, you may say that the ocean is treacherous and brings slick rain and you would be correct, but this felt otherwise. This felt intentional, as if a warning. More than once, the captain asked if we wished to turn around, but none answered affirmatively, so we pushed further into the storm. Water poured over the side of the boat to the point that I was assured of us capsizing, but then we broke through the wall of rain and saw in the distance a town.

It was Innsmouth.

Though there was no rain that I could see in front of us, my entire view of the town was shrouded in a somewhat soupy murkiness. Though I saw buildings through the fog and wet, they were blurry. Unclear. I would describe the view as dreamlike in a way. The sight was troubling, and I do not mind saying so. I cannot specifically pinpoint what caused such unrest within me. All I can say is that I felt as if I should have taken the captain up on his offer to retreat. However, before I was able to speak to him and change his mind, we pulled into the harbor and docked.

For better or ill, I was at the town.

I stepped off the ship with unsteady legs beneath me and had hardly placed a foot on the splintery wooden dock when a howling wind struck me and nearly drove me into the sea. The captain grabbed me by the elbow and ushered me to safety, as it was. I was grateful for his assistance, but noticed the ache in my stomach continuing as I surveyed my surroundings. My darling, how such riches as the gold given to me could come from an environment as this will eternally baffle me! I cannot understand how such a place even *has* residents to speak of, let alone any source of wealth. I should explain more, I believe.

Innsmouth, to put it gently, is a town direly in need of extinction. The buildings of the town are creaky, rotted, and what paint exists is peeling off in long, stained strips. The roads are not even slightly paved, as they have instead opted for permanently muddy trails for God knows what reason. The air stinks heavily of dead and decaying fish with a strong tinge of acidic saltiness. The town appears as if it is merely a shambling corpse of a place that once was only broken. All of this I could forgive, though, were it not for the residents. I cannot fathom how Lucien could have felt accepted and welcomed by these brutes. To a man, they are hideously ugly with wide faces, thick lips practically dripping with drool, large bulging eyes that look to and fro, and mere strings of wet, dark hair that dangle against their necks. Even their skin is repellant, as it appears to flake off despite the constant, unending dampness shrouding the town.

Beyond the abhorrence of their visages, though, they are universally unpleasant. They do not like me being here, as I do not believe they care for any sort of outsider, which further raises my suspicions about what Lucien could have possibly found here. By all accounts, he was a bright young man. Why on earth he would come to this damned place and attempt to make a living, to say nothing of the fact of being appreciative of what little value the place holds, well, it baffles the mind. What I *can* tell you, my love, is that any hope of celebrating Christmas in Innsmouth was crushed nearly as soon as I exited the train and walked the six miles to the town. Rather than a festive atmosphere with tinsel and lights and trees, I found nothing but muck, resentment, and damp.

The damp. My God, the damp. I mentioned it before, but it bears further explanation. It is omnipresent and sits on everything. *Everything*. It is almost like a curtain in the air or a blanket draped over the town. It is not exactly rain. There is no real precipitation to be found anywhere. Rather, it must be from the sea, because walking through town is much like treading through deep water in a way. The damp is cloying and sticks to your clothes and your skin and even to your eyes, making everything around you feel greasy. It is horrendous and I cannot fathom how the people in Innsmouth are able to tolerate the weather. I suppose I must admit, though, that the damp and dark of the town suits its inhabitants well. I feel myself repeating what I have already said, but words can barely describe the unpleasant nature of the Innsmouthians. Is that a word? I shall have to look it up when I have returned to civilization.

Though this is a place inhabited, it is nowhere near civilized. The people grunt and grumble as they walk, as if they are trying to speak but have lost the ability to do so. They shove one another if they collide and continue on their paths as if nothing had happened. No apologies. Just a growl or two and continuing to walk. I suppose that 'wander' would be a more appropriate term, for I do not ever see these people - such as they are - working or engaging in any sort of productive activity. Rather, they stumble groggily around the muddy streets and head to one tavern or the next. Drunkards all.

My love, I hope that I shall return quickly to you and our home. This place is abhorrent to my sensibilities and to anyone with a half modicum of decency. Why Lucien Weatherby saw fit to come here and, worse yet, reside here, I shall never know. You know, dove, that I look for the best in everything. I always search for a positive feature of anything, even that damnable solicitor job, because that is who I am. I wish to appreciate life for all its qualities. Yet, sweetness, I can find nothing redeeming in Innsmouth. I shall endeavor to return to you as quickly as I can. While the money from the Weatherbys would provide us a new life, I hardly think that I will be able to unearth their poor boy from the muck of this location. I do not wish to say he is lost, but if he is here, there is little hope that I will be able to retrieve him.

I miss you dearly and ache for the embrace of your arms.

You are my saving grace in this world, my love.

I adore you.

Your devoted Titus

December 27, 1921

My lovely Luisa,

I hope that this letter finds you well at your parents'. I hope that it is not too snowy where you are, but an appropriate level for the season. I miss you and cannot wait to be with you once more, though the timeline may have been extended slightly. Allow me to explain, if you will.

I must admit that, for lack of any better activity in this town, I did wander down to the bar on the lower level of the hotel in which I reside. I do not intend to become lost to drunkenness, but I had hoped that a glass of brandy would have taken much of the damp's power away. I hoped for too much, my love. When I asked the barkeep, an older man with craggy gray skin and a dull gaze, for the finest liquor he had in stock, he simply stared at me with blank eyes to the point of becoming uncomfortable. It became obvious that I would not find such finery in town, so I instead asked what alcohol he *did* have available. He mumbled something about local ale or wine, though it was difficult to decipher through the wetness spilling over his lips. He appeared half-drowned in a way. Though I had limited options presented to me, I knew full well that the hygienic conditions involved with whatever passed for beer in this place would have been nothing short of criminal in any other locale. I opted for wine, which ended up being a thick, dark vintage that tasted heavily of peat. It was not wholly unpleasant, though, and I found myself considering that there may actually be something in this place worth appreciating.

It was when asked for payment that I found some difficulty, as I presented the man with the appropriate currency but was met with only the same stare as before, though this time with a tinge of hatred lurking. I attempted to explain that this was how human beings purchased goods and services, as a gentleman does, but he began to bellow at me and point at the counter. As he did so, I noticed the curious nature of his hands and realized that I had been unkind to him. His fingers had thin webs between them and, coupled with the dead features of his face, combined to inform me that the poor man had been born with severe birth defects. He worked in this role because he was trying to better himself and, I must admit, I was ashamed of my judgmental behavior. We must look upon the unfortunate with pity and kindness, as our Lord would have done. Though my shame was well-earned, it did not solve the issue of my bill and what I needed to do to pay the balance.

In that moment, though, a savior came to me. A man - tall, swarthy, and dressed in clothes slightly nicer than the rest of the occupants' garb - walked over and placed a small chunk of gold on the bar between the two of us. He said that this would cover the balance of my tab within the duration of my stay here in Innsmouth and that I was to be provided every affordance possible to make me feel welcome. He turned to me and apologized for the bartender, saying that the poor fellow had indeed suffered many difficulties in his life and was provided employment here to give him a place in society. Such a curiously egalitarian and humanitarian motivation in such a small, ugly town! I will say that I did not hide my surprise as well as I had hoped, but he did not seem offended. Rather, he laughed and extended a hand to me, which I took gratefully. His grip was not slimy or slick, but firm and dry. He introduced himself as Harvey Marsh and that he was the official town greeter, seeing as he was a member of one of the founding families of the town.

As I faced him, I looked him over. While not traditionally handsome by any measure, Mr. Marsh was put together well and, though his eyes maintained the feature that I am choosing to call the Innsmouth Bulge, they were kind and filled with clear intelligence. He told me that they did not often receive outside visitors so, when one did arrive, the simple townsfolk had no social structure in place for being welcoming. In fact, he explained, most visitors to the town that they *did* receive were police or some sort of governmental workers bound and determined to stir up trouble. Naturally, the influx of authority created an air of hostility to anyone new, which I can understand. I am no stranger to the intrusion of the unwanted into our city, as you well know, my dear.

As he spoke, I found myself quite liking Mr. Marsh and, for the first time, could recognize a reason that young Lucien would have felt welcomed and wanted to the town. He was oddly charming and, over the course of another two or three glasses of wine, I told him of our life and who I am. I explained my discontent with my job and my frustration with being unable to provide you the quality of life that you so richly deserve. He listened patiently and nodded at the appropriate times. When I was finished, my senses were slightly inflamed, and I felt myself warm inside and out for once. He smiled and ordered another glass for both of us, though I tried to protest. He said, in a deep sonorous voice that I had not quite noticed before, that he understood my plight. Oftentimes, we find ourselves buried in dead ends in life and that it is up to us to unearth ourselves and grasp hold of opportunity when it presents itself. He told me that, many years ago, his grandfather Obed had done just that and brought immense wealth in the form of gold and fishing to Innsmouth. Apparently, once upon a time, the town was quite prosperous and lively, though you could scarce imagine such a thing looking at this godforsaken place now. He assured me that his grandfather had done much to make Innsmouth livable and wealthy, though he said something about an unnamed tragedy. He did not elaborate. I chose not to ask further, though that may have been due to my mind being clouded somewhat from the wine.

I asked him what he did for a living, and he was evasive in the way that only a man involved in unsavory business can be. Not that I have extensive experience with unsavory people, but in the solicitor position, you do come across the odd miscreant here and there. Still, Marsh seemed genuine enough when he spoke about caring for the town and wanting to restore it to its former glory. He alluded to some business deals he was hoping to renew in the future and asked if I knew anyone who would be interested and capable of helping him out in his goal. Well, far be it from me to self-aggrandize, my love, but I knew full well that I was such a man. I told him so and he seemed genuinely pleased at my ability and willingness to engage him. I told him that I would have to be provided access to the minutiae of his case, but he assured me that it would be no issue, though it would take him a day or two in order to put together a packet of material for me to read. Until then, he asked, would I be willing to be his guest at his manor rather than holed up in a squatter's paradise such as this hotel? My dear Luisa, other than your delicate voice, I have never heard anything so beautiful in all my life!

The last action of mine in this hotel room is to finish this letter to you. Once I have completed it and sent it off to you, I shall take my suitcase and trudge up the muddy hill to the Mason Manor perched at the top of the town. I feel that this is a step in the right direction, my love! I am excited for the future once more.

Please give your family my undying love. I am ever so grateful that they have taken care of you.

You are the fire within my heart, keeping me warm and alive.

Your darling Titus

January 1st, 1922

My sweet Luisa,

The happiest of new years to you, lovely. I hope that you rang in 1922 - a year I can scarcely believe! - with love and laughter and a glass too many of champagne. I do hope that you kept that monster Treadwell away from your virtue. Hah! I jest, of course, my dear. You would never enact such a betrayal on your beloved, of course. You are far too loyal and wonderful to debase yourself or our love with such tawdry behavior. All the same, please keep him away. I trust you explicitly. I trust him not a single ounce. Ah, but now is not the time to consider actions such as that. You must be on tenterhooks waiting for my next missive and update on our future!

Before that, though, I must put into words the progress of my search for Lucien. I must say that Mr. Marsh and his affairs have taken more of my attention than I should have liked. He was also less than delighted when I informed him of my intent to continue my original task in finding the lad. More than once, he made cryptic allusions to the town being a haven for those wishing to escape the world, though I do not believe he could be referring to Lucien. The boy, according to his parents, seemed quite taken with the town and had become revitalized by the change in scenery. That, to me, does not seem to offer the impression that he wished to hide away. Still, Mr. Marsh's disquiet in relation to my quest has complicated matters, particularly as I am indebted to him for my lodgings. As such, I have resorted to sneaking away in quieter times to resume the search. I have found precious little as a reward for my efforts, but I am endeavoring to continue. More than once, I have garnered a surprised expression from a resident before they returned to their standard glowering. For now, I must take pains to be careful.

As for the dealings with Mr. Marsh, I will admit that I was hoping that proceedings would have moved along slightly more rapidly than they currently have done. Mr. Marsh is a gracious host and his home pales in beauty only to you and you alone, but my patience wanes a bit more as each day brings no more progress than the day prior. It is through no fault of his, of course, that we have stalled in our endeavor. He has been frequently apologetic, though I can sense some frustration within him that he must continue to delay. His workers are not the most diligent, to say the least, in maintaining records with any degree of consistency, to say nothing of the quality of the records themselves!

What information does exist is like as not to be infected with the same damnable damp that pervades the town. Ink smears and runs and an entire month of numbers is lost in an instant. Some records have been burned. It is haphazard and I know that a man such as Mr. Marsh is strained to the very core of his being with tolerating such incompetence in his workers. Though, when I have repeatedly suggested that he relieve his workforce of their duties and replace them with capable workers from Boston, he has been exceedingly resistant. He holds some kind of loyalty to these useless louts and, to my concern, defends their actions and characters. Privately, my love, I believe they are his kin in some way. Perhaps not directly so, but certainly within the measure of cousins or in-laws. I understand loyalty in that context, but I cannot understand the depth of his defense. I recall that my father fired his own brother from the mill after *one* accident and did so without hesitation, apology, or remorse. It was warranted. There is no value in rewarding or ignoring an inability to perform one's duties, at least in my mind, but I am not in charge of his business.

I digress, I suppose, my sweet. Things are done in a certain way here in Innsmouth that I would not tolerate, but it is their home, not mine. It shall never be mine nor ours, in fact. I would never allow you to come to such a town as this. Your sensibilities are too delicate and deserve the purest of air and warmest of sun, not the moist, gray dullness of this place. Were it not for Mr. Marsh and his generosity, I would have been home with you days ago. I hope that I shall be able to return to you sooner than later. If progress is not made to my satisfaction within the next day or two – on either case – I believe I will remove myself from our agreement and find the first vehicle home and away from Innsmouth.

I miss you so dearly. My heart aches every time I think of you and of our life together. It is unfair that we must be apart, but I shall be with you soon. Until then, I will do my utmost to make the best of this situation and this home. Oh yes, this home! I quite nearly forgot to describe it to you. The manor truly is breathtaking, Luisa. Gold everywhere and smooth, dark stone, possibly even obsidian. It reminds one of the home of a magician or wizard from ancestry, funny as it sounds to say such. My room is luxuriously decorated and comfortable, though I find it slightly discomfiting to sleep in there at times. I feel as if I am being watched by some unseen force. Clearly, my loneliness is taking a toll on me. No matter, though. I will rest and tomorrow will be a new day, full of surprise and hopefully the improvement of our situation.

You are the breath in my lungs, Luisa. The blood in my veins. You provide me with life everlasting and I strive every day to be worthy of you. I try and I try and I will continue to do so until we are together once again. Please forgive this foolish man writing you his inability to fulfill your needs. I am trying.

You are that which brings me hope, my beautiful Luisa. I shall miss you more every day.

Your lonely, devoted Titus

January 6th, 1922

My beautiful Luisa,

I apologize for the lateness of this message. Things have been progressing at a rapid pace here in Innsmouth, though those are words I never once thought I would be able to put down onto paper. Mr. Marsh finally managed to acquire the necessary papers for me, and I found within them several legal claims that had not yet been pressed in court! For a man such as me, that is a goldmine and, for a man such as Mr. Marsh, it is a literal one.

You see, Mr. Marsh's grandfather formed a sort of alliance with a neighboring village or something of that nature, wherein they would provide gold to Innsmouth in exchange for other services which are unfortunately vaguely outlined in the documents. As near as I can tell, there was some sort of bartering in place involving townsfolk and movement. Perhaps the neighboring village was dying and required citizens? I cannot be sure as of yet and Mr. Marsh has been curiously silent on the matter. I have attempted to press him on the specifics, but he continuously moves the conversation back to whether or not the contracts are still enforceable. The lack of forthrightness from him concerns me, I shall not lie. Until now, he has been mostly remarkably warm and open, especially in contrast to the neighbors. While I do have some hesitation at his reticence, it is not enough to put me off the case. You know me, my love! I am like a bloodhound once on a trail - I refuse to bend or break from my task until it is complete.

This particular case is legally fascinating, if only because I am unfamiliar with the other participants in the contract. The contract does appear to be binding and signed by several members of Innsmouth past, including Mr. Marsh's grandfather Obed. However, the adjoining signatures from the other community are vague at best. Scribbles and signs, indecipherable even to a man such as myself. I asked Mr. Marsh - he insists I call him Harvey - about the community and he was as evasive as before, though he did inform me that the members of their clan, for lack of a better term, are even more secretive, reclusive, and resistant to outsiders than Innsmouth. Naturally, my curiosity was piqued, as was my concern for being able to ever enforce the contract. He seemed to not be bothered, though, so I thought it best to not push the subject.

After a few glasses of what I have labeled 'peat wine' (and have admittedly grown to love), however, Harvey grew quite loose-lipped when it came to the subject of what Innsmouth provided this other community. Over the years, he told me after a large sip of his wine, the town had provided citizens the opportunity to relocate and join this other group, something that was entirely voluntary. In return, this community, clan, what have you, gifted Innsmouth with raw gold, both ore and chunk, to be used economically within the town and to facilitate outside services if needed. The sticky wicket, so to speak, is that a generation ago, the gold ran dry and was no longer provided to the town. Understandably, this caused consternation within Innsmouth, many citizens of whom relied on the gold to maintain their stock of goods and to continue to fish with updated equipment. In retaliation, Harvey said, the citizens currently within the town were forbidden from engaging with the clan members until such a time as the bargain was upheld. Naturally, this created further issues as many of the citizens had returned from the clan with families of their own and had renewed their residence within Innsmouth. Such a demand would have unfortunately separated them entirely from in-laws or friends they had made. A deep divide in the town formed, with the old town leaders taking sides depending on what they believed to be most valuable. Obed and two other leaders chose the side of enforcement of the contract, while three others chose the side of maintaining relations.

The final tally was a tie and was broken by the mayor who, upon casting the final vote for the contract, was booed uproariously by those in attendance. These boos soon escalated into brawls and, eventually, a fight that poured into the muddy streets. Brother fought brother, husband fought wife, children fought each other. To hear Harvey tell the story was chilling, as he described the events clearly but with the eye of a young child of seven, the age at which he had been during the violence. As he spoke, his eyes drifted away and he was back there in that violent time, hearing the cries and spatter of blood and bone amidst the mud of Innsmouth. He returned quickly to the present, though, and brought with him a sort of embarrassed reticence once more. I believe he was slightly abashed at having revealed so much of the town's history, yet I found it fascinating! What a marvelous event that had never once been mentioned in larger cities! What a truly unique legend for a town such as this!

With all the contracts and discussions with Harvey, though, I will admit that I have not spent the needed time on the task put in front of me by the Weatherbys. I certainly hate to take their money without anything to show for it, but I could find no hide nor hair of him in the days before and after the legalese. I attempted to ask around but was met with stony silence at best. More than once, I was met with rubbery lips spewing a gout of black-blue spit at me with utter disdain. I have no earthly idea what could create such a tint to one's saliva, but if I must hazard a guess - as I must! - I would say that there is something in the ever-present dampness that likely affects their sinus passages, which in turn very well could produce such an ugly color. I pity them to an extent. While I shall one day soon leave this place and never return, they are doomed to stay here in this land with clouded sun. What a bleak existence. All the same, I shall not give up. Lucien must be here somewhere. It is simply a matter of unearthing him.

Darling, I must leave you for now, as Harvey has asked that I join him for supper in the dining hall shortly. There is one more occurrence, though, that I must tell you for it weighs on my mind. Harvey has spoken many times of his family and his fine daughters and sons, yet I have not seen any of them around. That is, until this morning. As you know my routine, I get up at the crack of dawn - or as near to dawn as I may muster - and engage in several minutes of rigorous calisthenics before breaking fast. I find that it invigorates the body and places me in a state of mental clarity. One habit that I must thank that odious employer of mine for instilling in me. Regardless, as I was stretching and about to begin my ablutions, I noticed that the door to my room had been left ajar. This surprised me, as I have made it clear that I value my privacy. Someone must have decided to go against my wishes. Quickly, I ran to the door and flung it open, only to see a shapely thigh disappearing around the corner of the hall. I chose not to pursue the Peeping Tom, as I was still clad only in my undergarments, but I was strangely compelled by the idea of someone having peered upon me with a lustful eye (near as I can assume). Not that I wish for any other than you, my dear! You are all I may think of in my private times. Still, there is something thrilling about it, is there not?

I hope to speak to you by telephone soon. Harvey assures me that the line is nearly repaired - some sort of nonsense about a flood washing away the lines and poles - and that I should be able to hear the sweet bells of your voice within a day or two. How I long for that moment! It has been far too long since I have heard you speak my name in such loving, reverential tones. I miss the feel of your breath on my face and the sound of your words in my ear. I miss holding you tight against all the evils of the world, content in the knowledge that I can and will slay any beast who comes within an inch of my love. You bring out the best in a man already as strong as I and you are to be commended, my dear.

I ache for you. I love you dearly.

Take care, my sweet.

Your loving Titus

January 8th, 1922

My loving Luisa,

I can stand no longer being away from your embrace. I have resolved to leave Innsmouth within a day's time. Much as I have appreciated Harvey's hospitality and generosity, the strangeness and guarded nature of the entire situation has unnerved me to my very core. Something is quite wrong in Innsmouth and I am positive, though I have no proof, that young Lucien is in some way involved.

Perhaps I should elucidate so as not to worry you. I know that your constitution, so delicate like a butterfly's wing, does not endure well the strains of tension or foreboding that even dime store detective novels create. Yet, this is real life, and the concern would be that much more bothersome for you. So, before I continue, let me assure you that I am perfectly intact and fine in every way. I have not been harmed or even hurt, save for my pride (and to hear your parents talk of me, that particular facet of my personality could use some reduction). Indeed, I have been treated uncommonly well for an outsider, though the townsfolk still merely tolerate my presence now. Still, tolerance is a far sight more appealing than active hostility, so those bridges have been crossed at least. A small victory for your Roman god, yes? Perhaps I wax hyperbolic, my love, but I do find that putting into words my concerns alleviates them nicely.

To the order at hand, then. I spoke in my last letter of having been spied upon by an unknown entity whilst in my bedchamber engaging in my morning ablutions. Though I could not identify the person, her leg emblazoned itself into my mind. My darling, have no fear of infidelity! I would sooner crawl with dogs and lay with pigs than touch a woman other than yourself. My Diana, my angel. I would never do something so untoward. I must admit, though, that something about the leg disappearing around the corner haunted me and still does to this very moment. At supper, I asked my host about what I had seen. I informed him that someone had been peering in on me and ran once they had been found out. He laughed, a strange burbling sound, and assured me that I had simply been visited by one of the more incorporeal visages lurking within the manor itself. He detailed to me some of the history of Marsh Manor, including the unfortunate deaths of many members of the Marsh Family. He spoke of his older sister and her bout with tuberculosis, his uncle and his accident whilst repairing the roof, and the terrible drowning of his young nephew during an outing at the shoreline. It did not occur to me in the moment to ask why on earth anyone would wish to visit the shoreline here.

I should explain the shore of Innsmouth a bit before continuing. You deserve to picture such a sight in your mind. Imagine the beaches in the Virginias but remove all sun and sand and joy from the equation. Replace them with a harsh, deadly feel. What little sand there is remains studded with stones and bones from various creatures that have dashed themselves to pieces on the shore. The rocks on the beach and near the water are razor-sharp and seem to move toward whoever goes near them, making merely walking down the beach a treacherous affair. The sea foam that washes ashore is also not pleasant and bubbly like that in South Carolina. There is no pure whiteness to be seen and no fluffiness to be found. Rather, the foam, though it may scarcely be called such, is thick, viscous, and stinks of decaying sea life. The color is grayish-green and the foam sticks to everything like glue. It adheres to your boots and trouser legs, soaking them with the stench of the ocean and refusing to let go, no matter how much you attempt to scrape it away with a stick or some such object. Fish that have been caught up in nets or caught by birds lay lifeless on the rocky shore, their flesh rotting away and being eaten by scavengers. The lifeless sockets of fish will reach deep into your soul and pluck at the strings, so I have found. On one unfortunate occasion, I went to the beach to clear my head and found a fox there, half-consumed, the fur clumped and matted with blood and other such fluids. Something had torn it apart and

[Editor's note: the rest of the paragraph was smeared with something dark and sticky, leaving it indecipherable.]

What I mean to say, my darling, is that the idea of a poor child simply drowning at the shore on an excursion did not sit right in my heart. I did not press, however, as such questions at a meal are beyond uncouth and I shall be *damned* if I allow behavior such as that to come from me in such an important event. Never the once shall you see me tell a bawdy joke or ask a question that does not belong! I am a gentleman and as such, I will behave as one. I informed Mr. Marsh - Harvey, yes - of this and he seemed amused at the forcefulness of my insistence. I choose to believe he found it charming and endearing rather than something to be mocked. He continued his story by telling me that the Marsh family, though greatly affected by poor luck and the ghosts of the past, will continue to grow and thrive with my help. I found it flattering, I must admit. To think that I am important enough to change the course of history, well, it humbles a man. It truly does. Not that I am in need of much humbling, despite the beliefs of your parents, but it places one on the precipice of creating a true legacy, which I desperately want for you and I and our future children. I want them to know their father as a brave man who saved an entire town from total ruination. Something to that effect, I suppose. We shall create the details later, of course.

After our dinner, I was so excited at the prospect of helping that I went back to my room and dove right into the documents again, though I perhaps should have waited for the next day. Regardless, I was curious about what I could do to aid my host and, lo and behold, something caught my eye once more. A word, a codeword maybe, continued to appear again and again within the document. It made no sense to me and still confuses me. It's the word *Dagon* or an abbreviation of *EOD*. It was not a word used as filler or legalese, however. It had meaning, though I am still unable to decipher exactly what meaning it *has*. It seems important, at least in my view, as it appears to be connected to the participants in the contract under consideration. I will have to ask more about that tomorrow.

However, the night grows late and the moon looms high above Innsmouth. It is exceptionally large and white, sending its beams shining down upon the town and the water in the bay. It is curious, in a way. The light is so bright that it plays tricks on the eyes. I could swear that I saw shapes swimming out in the bay, dark shadows against the moon's illumination. That is foolish, of course. No life seems to come near this place and that which does exist here would certainly not be foolhardy enough to go out swimming, let alone during the night. No, my dear, my eyes must be tired. With that, I must say goodbye and goodnight for now.

I love you. I miss you. I hope to be home with you soon. Though I promised only another day at the start of my letter, my curiosity has been piqued and I must see it through. I must be a man of my word, for without our words, what separates us from the wolves of the wild or the fish of the sea?

Please enjoy your solitude, my dove. Enjoy the house free of my botherations. You have earned your respite from me. I jest, of course! I know that you wish nothing more than for me to come home to you. Be patient, angel. Soon.

Your loving Titus

January 9th, 1922

My angelic Luisa,

What a turn of events has occurred here! Harvey has asked me to personally handle all the negotiations and enforcement of the contract myself! What an honor! What confirmation of my abilities! Truly, despite the lowliness of this town, there is something here that appreciates me for who I am and what I may do. No longer shall I be forced to tread the boards for that filthy firm at home. I shall be paid according to my effort and my skill, which as we both know is prodigious. Yes, my darling, I am certain that this place is where I am meant to be for the moment, at least until I see the finalization through. That begs the question, though, of whether you would wish to join me. As devoted as you are to me and I to you, I could not ask you to come to such a town of disrepair. The stink and damp in the air. The mud on the streets. The ugliness of the townsfolk in both presentation and personality. No, my dear. Innsmouth is far too undignified for one such as you. I wish for you to remain home for now. Attend your parties. Make your presence known in our social circles. Tell all who ask that I am away on exciting business. Mention the gold. Make *sure* you mention the gold! I know that such wealth will impress your friends and their husbands. Perhaps even enough to try to tempt me with employment better befitting my person! Goodness, Luisa. My heart is aflutter with such possibilities. I see the future sun beating down on us with favor!

Ah, yes, about the Weatherby boy. I nearly forgot! Though I mentioned before being slightly accepted here in Innsmouth, one or two of the townsfolk have, through no small effort on my part, become what passes for friendly with me. They will speak to me, if briefly, when I attempt to strike up conversation. One in particular, a Mr. Garbengl (a name of Turkish origin, I believe) has even gone so far as to share a bottle of peat wine with me once or twice. On the last occasion, he became intoxicated and confirmed to me that Lucien was, in fact, in the town, but that he was being hidden away for his safety and the safety of others. I had nearly convinced him to explain what he meant by that when another patron entered the tavern, and his lips sealed as tightly as if wax had been poured across them. Piteous luck, I say! I now know that Lucien is present in Innsmouth, though, so I am resolved to continue my search in secret. Between us, though, my love, I am not optimistic that the hunt shall end fruitfully for us all. Nevertheless, we endure.

Regarding our last letter and the word I mentioned - *Dagon* - Harvey struck a curious balance when speaking. He was reticent to speak much on things, but he was kind enough to illuminate some basic facts for me. According to

him, the abbreviation of *EOD* I mentioned refers to
The Esoteric Order of Dagon. It is an organization
of sorts here in Innsmouth and is exclusive to those
citizens owning land or businesses. He explained it
as being something similar to the social clubs of the
larger cities, only adapted for a smaller town. When
I asked what they did at their meetings, he laughed
and told me that they do nothing more than read the
minutes, bring up any concerns about the town they
may have, such as obtaining a permit to build an
extension to the bar, and then adjourn, play poker
and dice, and drink peat wine. Well, that sounded
like a right jolly time to me, so I asked if I would be
allowed to attend the next meeting on a provisional
basis or as his guest. He told me that he would need
to discuss it with the council that makes up the
leadership of the club, but he did not appear to be
much troubled at the prospect. Certainly, I would be
unable to join their ranks officially, as I am not a
citizen of Innsmouth, nor would I ever become one.
Still, developing a social reputation around town
beyond that of 'outsider' would be a boon to both
my comfort in this place as well as perhaps help me
carry out my duties and search more effectively.

While thanking him, I did ask what
Dagon truly was and it was then that Harvey
became tight-lipped, informing me that some things
are known only to townspeople. He apologized soon
after but reiterated that I would be better served to
focus on my task with the contract and documents,

as those require significant consideration and updating to reflect the current times. It was a fair point, and I was slightly aggrieved that I had caused him any consternation, but he reassured me that he was not upset nor offended and that he would discuss my attendance at the EOD meeting with his colleagues that afternoon. He then took his leave and left me to my work.

It was once I became focused on the work that I again felt as if someone or something were watching me. I knew that I had closed the door to the room in which I worked to avoid papers being blown by the occasional wind, but a breeze - cold and clammy - swirled into the room from behind me. The only way such a breeze could have occurred was if the door had been opened slightly. Someone was or had been there. I resolved, though, to not turn around and startle my observer. Having done so prior, I knew that whoever she was - a leg such as the one I saw could only be female - had a tendency to be skittish and run away. Perhaps if she mustered up the bravery, she'd enter in. I decided to wait and continue to focus on my work. Soon, I forgot that anyone had interrupted me, having become lost in the pages in front of me. Such fascinating details! *Dagon* seemed, for all intents and purposes, to be the community engaged with Innsmouth, though no direct confirmation could be found. That troubled me, as without specific mentions, it would be difficult to prove that money or gold was due to the town.

It was only when I felt a gentle touch on my shoulder that my mind was pulled unceremoniously from the puzzle and thrust into a state of minor botheration. You know how I get when I become entranced in my work! Nothing save an explosion will derail me, yet one touch did so. I turned and saw something that continues to confuse me, even as I reflect upon it. It was a girl, sixteen or seventeen years in age if I may guess, staring at me. She was clearly Marsh's daughter. She had his eyes - the typical Innsmouth Bulge - though hers were a curious blue-ish green, akin to that of the sea at noon. I would not endeavor to call her 'pretty', but there was a strange, otherworldly beauty in her features, from her eyes to her too-wide mouth and flat nose. The other feature of note her hair which was, rather than the stringy black wires of the typical Innsmouthian, a long, flowing mane of darkness that had the sheen of oil upon it. She looked at me and said nothing, instead running her hand across my face in a way far too intimate for our brief meeting. I reached to grab her wrist to stop her, and she pulled away, fright on her face. I quickly told her that she was in no danger or trouble and that I meant no harm to her whatsoever. She had simply startled me, and I asked for her name. She did not respond, instead merely cocking her head in a manner akin to that of a hound finding itself puzzling over something it had unearthed.

I introduced myself and bowed, as is customary for a gentleman such as I, but she still said nothing. Her silence was unnerving, and her gaze remained unbroken and curious. I asked if she needed anything from me with, yet again, no response. I was about to call for her father when he rushed in and ushered her out of the room quickly, muttering something under his breath in a language that I could not understand. Once she had left, Harvey returned and begged my forgiveness. That was, in fact, his daughter Amleragh - Irish, perhaps? - and she was not normally allowed out of her room as she required constant care. Her mother, Harvey explained, had been one of the citizens from that other town but was not capable of raising their daughter in an appropriate environment so, as her father, he took on the duty of bringing her to Innsmouth and providing her the home and medical or psychiatric care she needed. Shame filled his voice as he explained how it hurt him so to leave her locked away from the world, but that it was a necessary evil to prevent others from being harmed. I found it troubling that he mentioned his concern for *others* rather than his daughter, but it is no place of mine to truly judge a father doing his best.

I would be a great father, you know, my Luisa. I believe I have the temperament and ability to be

45

excellent. I am caring and nurturing and will be able to provide the life you all deserve. I shall do exactly that once we reunite as soon as possible. When that should be is the difficulty, I fear. If only I could figure out exactly what is happening in Innsmouth and with Lucien Weatherby, I may be able to return to your loving arms. Not knowing what I must know is vexing. Ah, but these are musings for another time, my love. I must continue with my work.

I love you with every fiber of my being. You are my peace.

I count the seconds until we are together once more.

Your adoring Titus

January 14th, 1922

My patient Luisa,

It has been too long since my last missive to you. I know this and I am apologetic beyond words. I hope you are finding your solitude relaxing, though I know you must miss me terribly. How I loathe making that heart of yours weep one single tear! I wish I could inform you delightedly that my tasks are complete here in Innsmouth and that I will be returning to you overnight, but alas, I cannot. My duties here, both to Mr. Marsh *and* to the Weatherbys, have conspired to extend my involuntary residency here indefinitely. Please, take heart, my angel and allow me to elaborate.

I found someone in town. No, not of a romantic nature! You need not worry. I would never besmirch either of us with such foulness. No, he is another outsider. A professor, in fact! I shall explain immediately.

I was taking a break from my work on the ever-increasing tangle that is the contract between Innsmouth and the village of Dagon and resolved myself to walk around town for a little while. It was the rare day where the sun came out and the damp had dried up, so I was eager to avail myself of the fine weather. Even the ever-present mud that makes up the streets of the town had somewhat dried into a

walkable form of dirt and stone! As I walked the
roads of the town, I noticed that very few
Innsmouthians were out and about and running
errands. It was as if the sun and warmth were
anathema to their being. Strange people becoming
stranger and the like. All the same, I found it
pleasant and, aside from the reek of hot fish
carcasses from the shore, it would even have been
something close to charming. Will wonders never
cease? I was in such a fine mood, in fact, that I
wandered down to the tavern near the shore to
indulge in a midday tipple over lunch. When I
entered the tavern, it was clear that - again - the
townsfolk were mainly nowhere to be seen. Only
the surly bartender was present and even he looked
more miserable than usual, which is saying quite a
lot. He demanded that the windows stay closed and
shaded and bellowed at me to shut the door behind
me.

When I reached the bar, I took a seat and asked
what was going on in town today. He grumbled
something about sunny days being bad for the
town's complexion and just poured me a glass of
wine before slapping down a plate with some sort of
fried sea creature and a pile of French fries on it. He
said it was compliments of the house and
grudgingly thanked me for my patronage. To say I
was shocked would be a vast understatement! The
meal itself was startlingly good. The fish was flaky
and moist and flavorful, with no trace of the greasy

sickness from the surf outside. Either they cleaned their fish exceedingly well or they found an alternative source of acquiring the meat. Regardless, I was effusive in my praise of the fish and, for a single moment, I could have sworn that I saw the man smile slightly before grunting and returning to his usual grumpy self. I did not mind. I had consumed a fine meal and was relaxing with my wine.

When the door opened a few minutes later, I assumed that some of the townsfolk had come to their senses and begun to resume their usual duties. It was not to be, however, as a middle-aged man with slate gray hair and a clean peacoat entered and shut the door quickly. He removed his coat and placed it on one of the hooks near the door before making his way to the bar and taking a seat next to me. His suit, a dark green, was impeccable and I feared for the health of the material when the weather in the damned town went back to the standard damp and muddy. He greeted the bartender by name, however, and was met with an actual toothy grin from the surly man. That was yet another surprise on what was turning out to be quite an interesting departure from my typical day. The man in green ordered a glass of the peat wine and looked over to me with a conspiratorial grin, as if he and I were sharing a private joke as outsiders, despite having never said a word to each other. I liked him immediately. Once he got his glass, he raised it to me and asked if I would toast with him to the mysteries of the world. Naturally, I accepted. What sort of man would turn down such a fascinating toast as that?

He introduced himself with a handshake as Dr. Henry Armitage from Miskatonic University in Arkham. You would be forgiven for not knowing of the town or the university - I was similarly unaware of either before speaking with the good doctor - but it is apparently a town of some repute in the academic world and maintains a sense of civilization. My love, it was like hearing that the Garden of Eden had opened its gates once more and had done so within an automobile's drive of this blighted seaside town! He said that he was Chief Librarian at the university - another well-read man, be still my heart! - and that he often made trips to Innsmouth in search of rare and esoteric books for the collection. Apparently, Miskatonic University has quite the archive of manuscripts both benign and malign from all over the world. My interest overflowed in that moment, and I am sure I sounded a fool as I explained my interest in books and readings and how I wished to write a book of my own one day. You know of this dream of mine, do you not? Did I never tell you? Oh, my love, what an error on my part! Yes, I have long since desired to write the next great novel to bring the masses to tears and be published across the world. It drives me daily. Of course, I keep it to myself most of the time. The world wouldn't understand my genius, nor would it be ready for such work.

Regardless, the good doctor seemed quite taken by my interest in his field and invited me to come visit Arkham and the university one day soon. I can scarcely believe it, my love! I will be away for even an afternoon from this blighted muck. The fresh air and civilization shall be invigorating, I promise you. I may even send for you in advance so that you may join me! Perhaps not. It is quite a journey from home, and you would find no joy in an afternoon of dusty tomes and academic pontificating. Those are not your desires, I know. We shall have to find you a knitting partner, I think! Company does wonders for the soul, let me assure you. I digress, of course, as I often do while speaking to you. How you make my mind wander!

As I was saying, Henry - he insisted on leaving the formalities behind as fellow scholars - had come several times to Innsmouth and had somehow ingratiated himself to the locals. I say 'somehow' teasingly, of course. The man is utterly charming and could sell ice to an Eskimo in the middle of winter! He told me of his interest in the town and some of the books owned and preserved by the Esoteric Order of Dagon - that name again! He wished to simply read them and transcribe what he could for the archives but had until that point been stymied by those in charge. Something about religious rites and the like, though who truly knows in a town such as this? He seemed convinced that, were he simply able to get the opportunity to plead his case, he would be able to convince the more reasonable members of the town to allow him to add the materials to the collection. I did not doubt his earnestness, but the task seemed a difficult one, especially for an outsider.

He then asked me if I would be willing and able to help him out in that regard. After talking with several of his more trustworthy compatriots in town, he had learned that another outsider had come to town and bent the ear of Harvey Marsh himself, even to the point of being allowed to lodge with him at his manor. I was unaware that such a thing was nigh unheard of in Innsmouth and, I must tell you, some air was lent to my self-esteem upon hearing that. I had not considered myself especially close to Harvey, but that was clearly incorrect! I told Henry that, yes, I would do my best to convince Harvey to consider Henry's request, so long as the invitation to Miskatonic still remained valid. He thanked me profusely, pumping my hand up and down multiple times with gratitude. Was there anything else he could do for me? Only then did I think back to the original purpose of my visit to the town and informed him of such.

He listened thoughtfully and nodded when appropriate. When I finished, he told me that he had heard about such cases before involving these smaller towns of New England. An enterprising young man or woman going to a place unfriendly to outsiders and disappearing was not altogether unheard of, particularly as finances became more dire over the years. He had even heard a tale or two about Innsmouth itself, though he was quick to point out that he did not traffic in gossip and that Innsmouth, once adapted to, was a place of great heart and potential. I will admit that I dismissed that idea outright. Innsmouth, for the few bright spots I have unearthed, is nothing more than a town that has already died but has not gained the good sense to accept its fate as of yet. I do not wish to be elitist or cruel. I see these poor citizens as unfortunate and living in a place where they are unable to truly succeed in life. They are bound by destiny to be unremarkable. I weep for them.

Oh, my tender heart. You have brought it out of me, my dove. You have freed me from the shackles of bachelorhood and instilled within me a compassion for all living creatures that growing up in my family never could. You have softened my hard edges and blunted the steel of my blade. For that, you are a savior to me. My Luisa. My grace. Your being apart from me is like having a limb removed and cast into the ocean. A piece of me is missing and you are that piece.

I have a surprise for you, though. While doing my work for Harvey, I came across a book he had carelessly left out. The title was something altogether foreign to me, but the cephalopodan feature on the cover, embossed and looming, pulled my attention to it and nigh forced me to open it. I could not read the text, as it was written in the same incomprehensible language as the title, but one phrase sounded so beautiful to me that I scribbled it down in my notebook before returning to my work. Something about it spoke to my soul and changed my heart.

I leave it here for you as a token of my deep, abiding love for you. Take it as *your* phrase, a mishmash of foreign words that is uniquely suited to the woman who has so fundamentally impacted my life and brought me to bliss unending.

My Luisa, *Iä! Cthulhu fhtagn! Ph'nglui mglw'nfah Cthulhu R'lyeh wgah'nagl fhtagn!*

I know not what it means. Speaking it aloud does nothing but mush the mouth together in ways entirely beyond that which I have experienced anywhere, but I believe it to be some form of Germanic origin. I shall have to ask the good doctor at our next meeting. All the same, it is for you. It belongs to you now, damn those who wrote it before! I hardly imagine that anyone will wish to lay claim to such a beautifully ugly phrase, so consider it a gift.

I must go for now, though, my lovely one. I still have much to do with this contract and convincing Harvey to meet with Henry. I gave my word and we must honor it. A trip to a civilized place! I can hardly sit still for the excitement it brings me! Books! A lack of dampness pervading everything! Food beyond that of seafood! To me, my love, it sounds nigh unto Paradise save one factor: you shall not be there. It grieves me, my love, and I shall mark it down as yet something else I needs must make up for when I return to you. It aches within me.

Take care of yourself, my dove. I shall return to you one of these days.

I love you beyond the depths of the briny ocean.

I am, as always,

Your loving, devoted Titus

January 19th, 1922

My Luisa,

I must admit that I find myself puzzled by the contents of your last message. While I was delighted, as I always am, to hear from you, the message did not sound as it usually does. The words and tone were different from who I know you to be. Tell me true: you did not write the letter, did you? The entirety of the message sounded as if someone else were writing it. Was it Treadwell? Did that scoundrel bull his way into your life and threaten you into compliance? Do not answer in the letter. You need not have your words used against you in written form. All I can do is hope and pray that you have found your way to safety. Perhaps back with your parents or with one of your society friends. Surely, they would take you in during a time of need.

I should return to you immediately. I should take the next boat out of this place or make my way to the train station. I should be by your side and freeing you from the machinations of such a perfidious figure. Yet, I cannot. Not yet. Would that I could, but my services are needed here in Innsmouth still and I must follow through with my promises, despite my misgivings and my fury. I did mention my concern to Harvey and, while he did understand my predicament, assured me that movement will be coming soon and that I may rejoin my family within the next week or two at most. So, for now, I must sit here and seethe rather than be with you, much as it pains me. Damn that Treadwell! I should have expected that he would interfere with our life together as soon as I was no longer physically present. A foul, predatory action to be sure! He shall soon face the wrath of my might in court. I shall extract my pound of flesh from him. For this, I shall swear on the grave of my sainted mother.

We should speak, though, of gentler things. My rage must ebb before supper tonight as Harvey and I shall have a guest - the good doctor Armitage! You read correctly. I, Titus, have once more moved mountains and the hearts of men to encourage such personalities to reach across the aisle in friendship and good will. Though Harvey was initially reluctant to consider even speaking with Henry, I appealed to his generous and rational soul and, in the spirit of cooperation and in acknowledgement of the services I have already rendered to him and the community, he agreed to break bread with our scholarly friend at dinner tonight. My hope is that they strike a pleasant accord and make an agreement to serve both to the best of their needs. I shall be there, so you need not worry. I shall use my wit and *bon vivant* nature to ensure that the conversation is peaceful and that the environment is suited to peace. I am excited! It has been far too long since I have had a meaningful meal with intellectuals of my own educational level.

Henry, as you may imagine, was delighted that I had managed to broker such a fine deal. He explained that he and Harvey had spoken at length in prior times, but that our mutual friend had been reluctant to engage Henry in even the most basic of compromises. I know quite what he means in that regard. I appreciate the generosity of my host, particularly regarding the lodging and food he has given to me without a second's hesitation, but the man is difficult to pin down. On some days and topics, he is gregarious, loud, and friendly. He will expound on any number of topics and seems to find great joy in bantering theories with others. He is giving to a fault and has been more than willing to provide me with nearly whatever I request. That he has not been elected mayor of this town yet speaks to his disinterest in holding public office more than any sort of qualifications he may lack. However, for all his positive qualities, the man is an enigma. At times, he is grouchy and tight-lipped. He will refuse to answer even the most basic of questions or will walk away from a conversation mid-sentence if he does not find the topic of interest or something he is willing to discuss. He is especially severe in his refusal to discuss much of the town's history, this *Dagon* community, the Esoteric Order of which he is a member, his family...really, anything that may give me a better idea of how to conduct my business here. I have long since given up the hope that he will extend me the courtesy of exploring his library, so I have been forced to sneak in at night or while working to see what I may find.

I am quite sure that Henry does not know of the existence of Harvey's library, for a mere meal would not sate his hunger given the extent of the collection that has been compiled in that room. Books ancient and curling from damp sit on thick oaken shelves. Piles of title-less tomes litter the floor and papers in languages common and unknown are scattered over the desk that Harvey must use for his own research. I wonder if I should mention the library to Henry at dinner. I would imagine that such a topic would create a tension unsuited to agreement or cooperation. Perhaps I shall tell him ahead of time. Or after? It is strange, Luisa. Somewhere inside me, telling Henry about the books and library howls at me that I have a moral duty to inform the man. How or why, I do not know, but the feeling persists. On the other hand, I have a debt as guest to Harvey to keep his secrets to some extent. I am, for the first time here, conflicted and wish desperately that you were here to dispense to me advice. You would know precisely what to do and how to do so, though both components I sorely lack at present. Perhaps that should be something I consider this afternoon rather than at this very moment.

Writing to you is so cathartic at times. Despite my concern about Treadwell and his influence, I cannot help but reach to you. You, even miles away, provide me a place in my mind where I may speak freely and find the truth of things. If you will indulge me, then, I have one more bit of news to share with you, if only to put it on paper and pull it from my mind.

I believe that I saw Lucien Weatherby yesterday.

I cannot be positive. Certainly not after merely a glance and double take. But something stopped me as I trudged through the re-moistened mud. It was a small house, white-painted, on the corner of one of the streets. It stood out to me because it seemed to be freshly painted. In a town such as this, anything fresh is an anomaly, to say the least. Though I had noticed it before, something compelled me to stop for a moment and gaze at the oddity. Just then, the door opened, and a pair of men came out. One was tall and broad, with a long, dark overcoat and slick black hair. The other was shorter, skinny - nearly too skinny, in fact, and had on a suit that appeared to be hanging from his bones. The taller man, I could not see his face, but the shorter man turned briefly to see what was around and I saw his profile. He had a pronounced chin and strong cheekbones, though a sallow complexion. Though I am not entirely sure, I believe that the man I saw was Lucien. He did not appear to be in any active distress, save his appearance, but he was ushered away quickly by his companion. I fear that the concerns of the Weatherbys may be founded, and that the poor lad is being held captive here in Innsmouth. I shall have to discreetly ask Harvey about it, though I do not expect to get more than a grunt and the basic 'some things are better left alone' speech he has given me many times as of late. I am not sure that he is tired of me yet, but I do feel as if my welcome is being worn out the more I explore. I am being safe, Luisa. Worry your head not! I am simply curious and indulging that curiosity as one does.

I shall message you once again soon. Sooner than this time.

I love you deeply, my sweet Luisa.

Your ever-faithful husband,

Titus

January 20th, 1922

Luisa,

My love and light. I am sending you this message with extreme urgency. Once you receive it, you must do as I request as soon as possible. It very well could be a matter of life or death, though likely not for me. I apologize for no flowery declarations of your beauty at the moment, but I am sore distressed and need to write this letter quickly and get it sent off before others decide to prevent that from occurring.

I shall cut to the chase, as it were. There is no doubt in my mind that the man I saw in town was, in fact, Lucien Weatherby. I saw him once more, this time peering from the window of the freshly painted house in which he resides (?). He is gaunt and pale, far from the hale and hearty young man I imagined he would be. His parents did give me some descriptions of what he looked like before they sent me off to search for him, so I could confirm his identity were I able to get closer, but I fear that attempting to do so would elicit some negative responses from those in town looking to keep him sequestered, for whatever reasons they may have. I should make this letter relatively short, but I must tell you how I managed to see young Lucien. I feel almost like a detective from a spy novel, though this is real life! Fanciful, I know, and dangerous to boot, but who says I am not allowed to enjoy myself a little bit even as I go through such strenuous moments.

Having piqued my interest the day before, I made my way to the street and took up position on a bench across from the house. I withdrew from my pocket a copy of the day's newspaper and began to feign reading from it. I am sure it looked slightly strange to the townspeople, but the fact they have a newspaper of their own while likely being illiterate appears strange to me, so the barrier between the outside world and them remains strong enough. I had no specific plan in mind - something I know will concern you, my love - but thought it prudent to simply wait around and see what I could see. I have run slightly aground on examining the contract and information, as Harvey has been singularly unhelpful with providing me with any more detailed information than he previously had given me. It seems almost as if he does not wish for me to complete my work, but that is a digression that can wait for a different time. Having the afternoon to myself and, being unable to peruse the library as he had taken up the room for his own studies, I was in possession of the luxury of time to wait.

Fortunately, or not, depending on how one wishes to look at the situation, I did not have long to wait. Perhaps a half-hour or three-quarters of an hour at most? Just when I was finding myself losing interest and wanting to curse myself for wasting such valuable time of my valuable life, I noticed a stirring on the upper floor of the building. Peering around my paper, I focused on the window to the upper right and saw that the curtains were moving to and fro, as if someone were pushing them aside. I continued to watch as the dark curtain was moved away and the face appeared. As I said before, the visage was gaunt and pale and nigh-skeletal, to put it mildly. It was, though, nearly undeniably Lucien, however. A birthmark on his nose was visible even at my distance and it was distinctive enough to put paid to nearly all my doubts. His eyes, as far as I could see, were wide and frantic in a way that most resembled that of a hare surrounded by hungry foxes. It was not haunted so much as hunted. There was fear there and I felt the urge to call out to him, throw something at the window, get his attention, anything! Instead, a large hand grabbed him by the hair and pulled him away from the window with great force.

My dear Luisa, I must admit that I am concerned in a way that I have not been in quite some time. The last occasion I can recall having this level of worry was when you fell ill last summer and needed to be rushed to the hospital to replenish your fluids. Why did you not drink water that day, my angel? It matters not at the moment, of course. I never wished to feel that worried again, yet here I am, sitting in my room at the manor, clothes still dark with the dampness from the air, hair slick against my face, writing you to ensure that I will get these words out before I do something foolhardy. You know that is not my way, my dove! I must plan out my actions and I believe this situation is no exception. In fact, I would dare say that it matters even more now than it has before. I do not know what forces have conspired to force and hold young Lucien Weatherby in seclusion but, even if the forces are the one large man with him, that presents a problem for me far beyond my capabilities. I shall have to find an ally in town to work with to help uncover whatever may be happening. Perhaps Dr. Armitage - Henry, yes, I know - would be willing to assist me in formulating some way to gain information or perhaps even rescue the young man from his captors.

What a thrill! I know, the morbidity of such a statement is unlike your gentle Titus, but being out in the world and finding and observing those that may do ill to others is invigorating in a way I cannot quite explain, I am afraid. It is so unlike anything I have known before in our town. For so long, we have been prim and proper and behaved ourselves by the standards of society. As we should! As all should. It is neat and clean and tidy and absolutely everything I have ever wanted. I still do want that with you, my love. But there is something exciting about seeing the world as it is in all its dirt and muck and blood and death. Something primal. Unique, perhaps.

I do go on, my dear. I must be frightening you something awful. Rest assured, angel, that I am the same Titus of yours that last you saw. I have my heart and my mind, neither of which can be taken from me even by force! Those both belong to you, my darling. I should go, however. I shall talk to you -

[Editor's note: Something was scribbled away here, almost as an afterthought. Nothing could be recovered save the word 'vermis'. That is Latin for 'worm', I believe. Curious.]

Wait, I had a task for you. I recall now! Yes. Yes, my sweet messenger, I require that you go and speak to the Weatherbys. Tell them that their son is in grave danger and that they would do well to commission someone - anyone - to rescue him. Any such task is far beyond my capabilities, I am afraid. I am not a fighter. No, my sweet, I am a lover and you know that all too well. My, that was quite indecent of me! My deepest apologies, dove. I shall keep our intimate time secret as the grave.

I shall see you soon, I hope. I feel the danger dissipating as I speak to you!

Your loving Titus

January 25th, 1922

My lovely Luisa,

Such a time I have had these last few days! The conversations! The knowledge! The meals!

Ah, but of course, to you first. How are you faring? I am sure my last letter sent you into a condition of sorts and, for that, I am sorry. I do hope you spoke with the Weatherbys, though. What do I say? Of course you did! You are always so faithful and true. Such an act would be nothing out of the ordinary for you. I hope I did not worry you too deeply, love. It was merely an overreaction to half-seen images and the like. You know how I get, always jumping at shadows, yes? Your scaredy-cat Titus? Is that me? I wonder. It does not feel quite right, but so be it.

You should visit Innsmouth one of these days, my darling. We will take a trip up to Arkham and Miskatonic University! I am beyond eager to wander those sacred halls once more. To tread the cobblestones and smell the fresh air. To inhale the dust of a thousand ancient tomes and feel the crispness of intelligence once more! I must tell you of my trip before anything else.

I had managed to broker a deal between Henry and Harvey - did I tell you that already? - for Henry to be able to look at one of the books belonging to the EOD (Esoteric Order of Dagon, as you recall) and the good doctor was so thankful that he asked me to return with him for a couple days to Arkham and Miskatonic while he found other arrangements for his classes. It would take him a couple days because, according to him, Miskatonic has a chronic problem with time management. Regardless, he wanted to return to Innsmouth shortly, but wanted me to come along with him to the university. He knew I was excited to get out of Innsmouth - who would not be? - and would be glad for the company, as he said. Not needing much but a few sets of clothes and my accessories, I packed with as much speed as I could muster. Oh! There was another strange instance. Goodness, I jump about frequently, don't I, my love? As I was saying, I was about to leave to join him when I was stopped by Amleragh, Harvey's daughter. She said nothing, as was her custom, but merely placed a hand on my forearm before quickly scurrying away. It was a strange gesture and one altogether too familiar for the brief moments we had even seen one another. I have a suspicion, my dear, that your beloved Titus has an admirer! It is and shall always be unrequited, of course, but the tenderness in her hand made me ache twice as much for your touch. We truly must bring you out to Innsmouth, my angel.

Henry had managed to procure a taxi - somehow! - so we did not need to bundle ourselves into a train or, worse, a boat. Instead, we rattled down the muddy road until we mercifully reached more favorable roads, at which point the shaking and rattling we had experienced smoothed out and we were able to chat amiably for the rest of the journey. He is a fascinating man, dear Luisa! I believe you two would get on famously. He is charming and erudite and utterly enraptured with the idea of finding, or rather unearthing, lost knowledge. He spoke quietly about the collection of books held deep and privately within the university library. Books from all over the world and written in languages familiar, foreign, and unknown. Books small and unassuming. Books bound in human skin! How deliciously morbid, would you not agree? Henry spoke of these books with a reverence typically seen only in the most solemn and dedicated of churches. In direct contrast to those places, though, these books are not holy. At least not to anyone in the civilized world. Well, that we know of, I suppose. He mentioned these books being kept under lock and key within a room *also* bound with a lock and key, though that seems a bit redundant, unnecessary, and frankly amusing to me. How dangerous can books truly be? Knowledge is good - all knowledge! The more we learn about the world, the more we can find ways to live better lives for all. Henry, though, does not subscribe to the same optimistic view that I do. He cautioned me to be exceedingly careful if I were to see those books and, in fact, said that I would not be allowed to view them without being accompanied by either him or Dr. Llanfer, a colleague of his. Welsh, perhaps, given the vestigial L in his name. While I was not pleased by the lack of freedom, it was not my place to make a scene. After all, I was a guest and being provided access to privileged information *at all*. Complaining about the circumstances around that access would have been gauche and ungenerous of me. So, I agreed to take care and he seemed appeased by this.

It was strange, Luisa, but as we spoke about the books, he almost grew darker in a way. Not physically, not permanently. Perhaps in a spiritual sense. Lines on his face appeared, his eyes grew shadowy and sunken, and even his hair whitened. Were I a man who believed in haunts or ghosts, I would have described him as *haunted* but that is laughable on every level. When I agreed, though, he smiled and all the effects I had been imagining - because they were simply my brilliant brain extrapolating his old age! - disappeared as if they had never existed. It was quite remarkable, dear! You two would get on famously. Did I write that already? Surely not!

Ah, yes! The university! What a stunning architectural wonder! The campus is wide, expansive, almost too large for the number of students and faculty on the grounds. The buildings are lovely and made of a dark, sleek-looking stone that is beyond that I have ever seen before. When I asked Henry about the material, he replied that he did not know but referred me to a Professor William Dyer if I was curious. Perhaps I shall look him up another time. Geology *has* always fascinated me in a way I could not elucidate. Yes. Perhaps I shall do just that. As I was saying, Henry led me through the campus until we reached a massive building. It was twice the size of all the others and the doors were made of a beautiful cherry-colored wood with large brass handles. My expression must have given my appreciation away, since Henry chuckled and told me that I was far from the only one to be taken aback at the beauty of the Miskatonic University Library. Wait until you see the inside, he told me with a laugh before pulling the doors open with a low, rumbling creak. It sounded like a dungeon door opening, if I may be honest.

My love, you have never seen such magnificence! The library is tall and has a beautiful glass ceiling, something I had only seen in New York. There are three stories, all circular and facing out into a massive open hall in the middle. The hall is filled with desks and chairs for students to inhabit while studying and a few of the members of Miskatonic University were doing just that. I noticed two tables piled high with books and, surrounding the books, several haggard-looking students with disheveled clothes. Henry whispered to me, in a volume only a true librarian could muster, that it was midterms and studying was of the utmost necessity. The importance was so much so, in fact, that the library had temporarily adopted a twenty-four-hour schedule in which there would always be a librarian around, but students could come and go as they pleased, even if the time were well into the morning hours. I found that quite charming and a kindness that I did not experience with my own schooling, as you can well recall. Henry explained that the rigor of the courses provided by the university was such that it would be a disservice to the students to not allow them as much access to information as possible. Once again, that warmed my heart and I ached at the thought of having attended such a caring institution rather than my own. Still, it is not like me to wallow in nostalgia, of course, so I nodded and we continued along our tour.

The shelves! My God, the shelves, Luisa! Floor to ceiling on every level and packed entirely full of tomes and papers and manuscripts. Every subject one could possibly imagine was there, from basic mathematics to the most obscure historical documents. Henry even pointed out a section under construction that was designed for human sexuality, though he cautioned that the layout of such a section was going to be different so as to prevent any prurient activity (chiefly onanism, I gathered) from occurring within the shelves. Though the expense was higher, the necessity remained and I did not find myself inclined to argue. I was young once, as were you, and more than once, I recall us finding ourselves lost to our passions in some hidden-away nook of an academic building or two. That is not worth thinking about right now, of course.

As we went on, I found that I was growing weary of the mundanity, beautiful though it was, of the library and the knowledge it provided to all. Somewhere deep inside of me, I felt an itch pulling me toward the third floor. I imagine I must not have been subtle about this, as Henry laughed - quietly, naturally! - and informed me that we were nearly at the place he knew I wanted to be. The place that all who are not students want to be, that brings scholars and curious minds from all over the country and world. The place where the darkest and most forbidden of knowledge lurks. The special room of esoterica. Yes.

Luisa, my love, there are no words to properly describe the feeling I had when we reached our destination. Excitement and nervousness and a soupcon of fear mixed in my stomach like a fine dinner. As we approached, I could feel my nerves twist into knots for no reasons that I could properly identify. I wanted to run, yet desperately wanted to stay. It was quite a fascinating combination of emotions, I must say. It is no stretch of the imagination to say that turning the corner to see the entrance to the forbidden books was akin to the experience of walking into a church for the first time, intend on marriage. I would believe, anyway, that it will be similar when we are wed. We are not yet bound in marriage, yes? Forgive me. The memories of the experience have washed away much that I know to be true. I shall explain momentarily.

The door was a deep mahogany with handles of what I believed to be steel but was told were actually a mix of iron and silver. Into the wood were carved symbols I did not recognize. I was told they were signs of protection from various religions around the world. Christianity. Buddhism. Islam. Any number of Eastern religions. Even some Norse runes. As Henry so eloquently put it, it was better to be overly cautious and to cover every possibility than risk the chance that none would be effective. Against what, I asked, but he was evasive, instead pulling an ornate bronze key from a necklace close to his breast and unlocking the door with a heavy thunk. Look at me, being poetic! Your Titus, a poet. How novel!

Inside, the room was innocuous at first glance. The room was not exactly what I was expecting, though I cannot be sure of what expectations I had. Perhaps chains on the walls to leash devils? Circles of blood or salt, maybe. Instead, there sat a table - albeit one of finer quality than those scattered throughout the library proper - and four chairs, all located in the middle of the room. It looked, for all the world, to simply be a study room for students. That is, it did so until one looked at the walls of the room. Glass cases, each individually spaced and locked, covered the available space. Some containers were filled with paper or books. Some were empty. A scant few were covered up with what seemed to be red velvet, which I must tell you piqued my interest to quite a spectacular degree. Henry welcomed me to the room, ushered me inside, and locked the door behind us. He told me, matter of factly, that the room was to be locked at all times, day or night, aside from the brief moments when someone entered or exited. He even said that he wished that the university would have allowed him to invest in a secondary door so that there was a failsafe in case of some event happening, but that he had been denied on every single occasion. The bitterness in his voice was palpable and made me wonder exactly what was so dangerous.

He said that there were things in the room that threatened the whole of life itself. Not just the library or the campus or even the town. Everything. Everyone. Every single atom that has ever been or shall ever be. How is that possible, my love? How can something exist with that immensity of power? I asked him and he told me that there are things beyond our capability of knowing and that a rare few humans have compiled many of such into a physical form. He called them fools and greedy, gluttons for knowledge only sated by experiencing moments beyond reality. He began to rant but stopped himself momentarily, apologizing. He had had a devil of a time simply getting approval for this room itself, to say nothing of acquiring the books, and that he was tired of having to justify himself and the expenditure of resources and finances to place such objects somewhere they could be safe. Controlled. Observed. Destroyed, if need be.

I did not argue with him. It did not seem my place and he had been kind enough to allow me access to such a hallowed sanctum only after knowing me a scant few days. The idea of such knowledge being destroyed, though, troubled me. I am not ashamed to admit that. I believe and have believed that all knowledge should be available to the wider public. Misuse of ideas is only reserved for the worst of humanity, such as those controlling the most recent war in Europe. The average layman will not have the mental capacity to utilize higher-level concepts for ill or harm. At best, he will simply not comprehend the words he is reading and will toss the book aside in favor of pablum more palatable to his being. Fortunately, people such as that will never know of the existence of the room, much less of the books therein.

I digress in such a fashion, my dear. It is far too long a letter. I shall send this and start immediately on another missive for you! You may call this a first draft, if you like.

I love you, my angel.

Your devoted Titus

January 26th, 1922

My darling Luisa,

To continue from my previous letter! I apologize for this coming to you later. I found myself distracted reading over my own words. How erudite a man may be when his heart is stirred to passion! As disdainful as I may have been about my place of schooling, it did teach me the value of words and how best to use them to beautiful effect. I envy you, dove. You are able to read stories from your beloved such as may have been printed in the newspaper itself! Perhaps that waxes slightly too self-aggrandizing. My apologies. I continue!

While I was in the room with Henry, he asked me if there were any specific books I was interested in observing, though not reading. He cautioned me that being anything other than entirely prepared for reading through the material would be disastrous for my mind. I found that a bit hyperbolic, but he was earnest enough. Teasingly, I asked if I could see the most dangerous object in the room. I did not know how often I would get the opportunity to enter such an esteemed place, so there seemed to be no point in me asking for less than I could possibly receive. To his credit, Henry did not refuse me outright. He heaved a sigh that seemed to hold the weight of the entire world within it, but he nodded. He told me that he expected as much and that the specific book tended to be the most requested *and* most rejected by the staff.

Henry walked over to the other side of the room, to one of the velvet-covered boxes. This particular box was located as far from the door as possible and seemed to have something bulky underneath the fabric. Indeed, when Henry gently removed the sheet from the box, I saw the reason for the shape. There was an extra layer of security around this specific box: a thick, iron chain with a large, heavy-looking lock binding the box shut securely. I wondered what could possibly warrant such control but did not speak my curiosity aloud. Henry was more serious than I had originally thought. I could see a light sheen of sweat on his forehead, despite the room being relatively cool. From his pocket, he withdrew a heavy iron key, inserted it in the lock, and turned it with no small amount of effort. Something creaked and protested before the lock clinked open and dangled from the chain. He grabbed the open lock in such a way that could almost have been akin to how one holds a rosary before placing it on the table and beginning to unwind the links from around the box. I offered to help but he told me to stay where I was, so I obliged. After a minute or so, the chains were off and thudded to the floor. The room was uncarpeted and the sound they made when landing on the hardwood nigh on echoed through the entire building! Henry, now looking pale as a fish belly, reached over with a trembling hand to the latch on the box and flipped it up.

Before opening the box proper, he asked me if I was sure that I wanted to see what was inside. The tone in his voice was near-on pleading with me to say no and, I will admit, I considered it heavily. Something to elicit this amount of fear from a man who walked carelessly through a town as ominous as Innsmouth surely would have been something terrifying beyond reason. Still, I had come this far, and my curiosity was inside my heart like coal from a roaring hearth. I nodded and he sighed, shuddery and deep. Before he opened the box, though, he reached into a nearby bin on the wall and pulled out two sets of white gloves. Tossing me one set, he told me that I had to put these on to protect both the book and my skin. By this point, any thoughts of arguing had dissipated, and I did so without complaint. The gloves were thick and woolen, but I could move my fingers well enough. Once they were on, Henry grabbed the handle of the box and slid it open. This surprised me, as I assumed there would be hinges on the door, but it was more like one of those sliding Japanese doors. You know the kind I speak of, yes, dear? I surely must have described them to you before. Regardless, you can certainly use your imagination!

He reached in and grasped something in his hands before pulling it out with a grimace. Holding it away from him, he set it down on the table and breathed heavily. He motioned for me to take a seat at the table, and I walked over, something itching inside my head. It was as if I had been bitten by something within my brain, like a fly or a nit. I ignored it and, when I reached the table, I found myself disappointed at the innocuousness of the object in front of me. It was merely a book, bound in leather, with yellowing pages and something scribbled on the cover in black. He called it something ridiculous. I believe it was the *Necronomicon* or the Book of the Dead. He told me that it came from the Middle East from centuries ago, written by a mad Arab named Al-Hazard. Perhaps? You know the sort of name. For the next couple of minutes, he explained to me the provenance of the book. From where it came to those who were in possession of it before the university managed to acquire a copy. According to him, this specific copy was one of extremely few and rare legitimate copies of the book. He explained that, to prevent the material in the book from reaching the general public, many duplicate fakes were produced and distributed to libraries and the like. He called it a precautionary measure.

My love, you could have cut the tension in the room with a butter knife. How could such a book exist? How could something so dangerous actually *be*? I asked Henry those very questions and he uttered a noise that I understood to be the closest approximation of a laugh he was able to create. He said that I was asking questions that, in any other context, would have been legitimate and precisely what should be asked. In this specific instance, that being both this book and the rest of the tomes in the room, the more accurate line of inquiry should be how they could be destroyed. I must say, love, I was appalled. Here was a man, a librarian, a scholar, someone bound to literature and knowledge for the entirety of his adult life, outright encouraging the destruction of information! This was beyond the pale and I told him so, but his reaction was not one of defensiveness, but of weariness. He told me that my rejection of the idea was, on its face, noble and one worthy of propagation. He agreed with me that knowledge for its own sake needed to be preserved and provided to the public in order to create a world filled with intelligence and compassion and empathy and other rubbish like that. It was in the case of these books, though, that the world is better served by forgetting that they have ever existed.

The question, then, that lingered over everything was simple: why was this particular book, this particular room, so dangerous to humanity? What horrors lurked within the pages locked away here? What darkness could come forth from nothing but ink and parchment? Henry touched the Necronomicon with a gloved hand and said that I was attributing normal features of literature to the power contained within the glass boxes of this chamber. For instance, this book, this seemingly harmless object in front of us, was not bound in basic leather as I originally had imagined. He told me, with no pretense or falsehood, that it was in actuality bound in human skin. I wanted desperately to disbelieve him, my angel. I wanted him to be telling me something macabre to elicit a horrified reaction from me. I wanted him to be playing a childish prank on me. Looking into his eyes, though, I saw nothing but veracity in them. This tome, apparently full to the brim with dark words, had been constructed using the dried flesh of human beings. As I peered closer at the book, my horror was confirmed as I saw miniscule pores speckling the binding.

Where did this come from? I asked Henry and he hesitated. He told me that he both couldn't and wouldn't reveal the source but confirmed that the book had originated with that scholar in the Middle East. It had been passed from merchant to scholar to magician to the deranged and back again several times over. It never existed in one place for too long, though. Someone inevitably opened it to peruse the contents and unleashed upon their lives something that they would be unable to control. Something terrible and beyond us. When did this book come to Miskatonic? Henry was unsure, but it had been property of the university for well over a decade now which, in the book's timeline, was the equivalent of several lifetimes. The next question I had, as I'm sure you have had as well, was of course to ask whether he had taken a look at the contents of the tome. Henry did not speak for what felt like an hour but was likely only a minute or two as he contemplated the question. Ultimately, he told me that he wasn't sure. How could that be? He said that the temptation had always been there, lurking in the back of his mind like a misplaced toy, but he had always held firm to his refusal.

One night, though, he consumed far too much whisky - the finest from Scotland itself - and apparently stumbled into the library and made his way to the top floor. Drunkenly, he fumbled with the keys and made it into the room. It called to him. A voice in his mind. Dark and deep and terrible. It spoke to him, begged him to speak aloud the words within the book. It told him of riches and power beyond his wildest dreams. It promised a seat at the right hand of the great conquerors that would be set free. He shut the door behind him and locked it, stuffing the key back into his pocket. The voice grew louder, nigh on deafening. It demanded obedience, acquiescence, fealty. It told him that he would be the herald of a new day and new era in history. He reached for the lock to the case and then the liquor overwhelmed him. He woke up in a pile on the floor the next morning with a head full of splinters, a mouth full of cotton, and a worried half-recollection of the night before. He did not, however, have an unlocked case in front of him. His body had saved him.

This sounds ludicrous, I know, my sweet. Such evil does not exist in the world. Not truly. Even those warmongers that thirst for blood and violence are motivated by some thought of good, I can hear you say, and I will agree with you. To a point. But Luisa, my light and my love, there are such things that we cannot understand. We cannot know the heart of the great jungles in Africa and what lurks within their tangled weaves. We cannot know what looms at the bottom of the ocean, buried deep in the black, cold water far beyond anywhere we can reasonably expect to ever reach. We cannot know what exists beyond the sky, out in the night above us, nameless and endless. My love, if we cannot know that evil does not exist in those locations, how then can we truly know that evil - pure, bone-deep evil - does not exist in a more tangible form? I cannot say for certain. I once thought I could. Believed I could. Was in fact sure of my ability to cast the idea of evil down to the depths with Satan himself and repudiate the idea that it exists around us in anything abstract. I was sure. I was so sure.

Luisa, I am no longer sure. I cannot be. For I gazed upon that book and saw the scribbles on the cover turn from a blur of black ink into a single word: *Necronomicon*. Clean and understandable, the word resonated within my heart like a drum struck by a stick but echoing with a pain that transcended time and space itself. No, not pain. That is not the right word. Something other. Something dark. Perhaps it was fear. Yes. Fear. Not fear for my physical safety. Not really. Well, perhaps. More so, though, I found myself in fear for my mortal soul. My love, you and I have attended church regularly enough to know that you and I are faithful people. We may slip now and then on our journey to Paradise, yes, but that is the burden of all humans, is it not? In the presence of the book, though, I found myself in doubt of regaining the path at all. Now that I consider it more carefully, that doubt extended to being in proximity to all the books in that room, all of which Henry patiently pointed out to me. *De Vermis Mysteriis*, or *Mysteries of the Worm*. The *Dhol Chants. The Book of Eibon. Unaussprechlichen Kulten* by a German scholar, von Junzt. Others that had no names or labels upon them. All these texts forbidden or dangerous. All hidden away from the eyes of all but the most educated or worthy humans. All singularly possessed of a kind of knowledge beyond that of understanding. And of course, the centerpiece, the keystone, the *piece de horreur* as it were, is the book created - birthed, nearly - by that mad Arab centuries ago: the *Necronomicon*.

My darling Luisa, while I was in that room, I came to one singular conclusion: these books should be burned. I do not say that lightly. I value

knowledge and literature more than human life at times. It is a failing of mine, I know, but to this point in my life, I have been entirely invested in propagating information and thinking. Now, though, my sweet, I believe in nothing more than the destruction of such horrific knowledge. Worse than the idea, my dove, is the concern I have about such books. You see, I suspect that, if such actions were possible, that Henry or his peers would have already done so and with gladness in their hearts. Such artifacts would have been put to the flame without a moment's hesitation and the world itself would have been blessed by the holiness of the cleansing fire. In fact, as Henry pointed out and named the various books, I saw one particular text
- *Thaumaturgicall Prodigies in the New-English Canaan* by a Reverend Ward Phillips - with edges dark and crisped as if having already been set aflame at some point. Whether it had been retrieved or simply refused to be destroyed, I could not speculate.

Night comes, my angel. I shall continue this tale in my next letter. Know that I love you beyond my ability to think logically.

Your beloved Titus

January 27th, 1922

My darling Luisa,

Where was I? Ah, yes. I was waxing poetic on the nature of the books in the collection at Miskatonic University. I am afraid that I left you awaiting the conclusion at perhaps the most inconvenient point. Before I continue, please, I ask that you respond whenever you can. It has been several weeks now since I heard from you, and I worry for you. Have you been harmed in any way? Have you had your life consumed by another man? I could not bear to think of it. Please, my sweet, if you hold any love in your heart for me still, reply to this letter to let me know that you are still my devoted one, safe and sound, hale and hearty, healthy and happy. Well, as much as you can be without my presence, of course.

Yes, the story. I have not forgotten. I will admit that I was taken aback by all that I saw in the room. The history. The knowledge. The darkness pervading the very wood of the floor and ink in the texts. All of it affected my sense of reality and I sat down in the chair nearest me. Henry was not unsympathetic. He explained that a place such as that would often overwhelm new visitors, even admitting that every now and then, he still felt the dread sitting on him. He told me not to worry and that these books were being maintained and protected precisely *because* they were so dangerous. They would not allow just anyone to come in and look at them. He then asked if I wished to read a page of the *Necronomicon*.

I found myself aghast at such a suggestion posed to me with the sort of nonchalance in his voice. I told him to repeat himself and he did so, telling me that there was very little danger in doing so. You will notice, my love, that such a statement directly contradicted everything he had told me to that point and the uneasiness in my stomach grew. I looked at his face, but something there prevented me from focusing on him. I find it difficult to describe even now, but it was as if I were looking into fog and seeing him sitting there. As if my eyes had clouded over with drink or exhaustion. I knew - I *knew* - that attempting to read the book would damn me, but a force unlike any other compelled me and I reached forward. He did not stop me, instead simply smiling at me through the smoke around his head. With a hand not of my own, I touched the cover and felt the roughness of the skin even through the glove on my fingers. I grasped the cover and opened it, exposing the first page of the book. A glimpse of ink, black as clotted blood, and strange symbols drawn (carved?) into the page and then the cover was slammed down by Henry.

He was horrified and stared at me with wide, frightened eyes. He asked me what the hell I was doing (using a more explicit vulgarity) and I could not quite explain. I told him that he had asked me to open the book and read from it, an accusation he vehemently denied. He said that we had been talking and then my eyes glazed over, and I opened the book before he could stop me. I told him of the fog around his head and he assured me that no such thing ever happened. That I had been fooled by the presence of the book. That I needed to clear my mind. He would not be showing me this or any other book right now. I had proven that, while a dutiful learner, I was not willing to abide by the rules put in place to protect everyone. I could not argue with him. Even with the slight glance I had taken at the first page of the book, something had lodged itself in my mind. Something heavy and throbbing, like a shard of glass. No, not glass. Something sharper. Obsidian.

I remember little of the following couple days. Even as I walked around campus and the town of Arkham, I could not appreciate the beauty as I once had. I could not imagine the softness of the grass or the tenderness of the food. I could not picture much of anything except the words and symbols on the first page of that damned book. I could not make heads nor tails of what I had seen but the fascination drew me toward the library again and again. I would stop myself before I went too far - I had no key to the room, of course - but would frequently find that I had opened the front doors or entered the lobby.

On one specific occasion, I was on the third floor, staring at the door, when I was shaken out of my trance by another librarian. He was a younger fellow, and I did not get his name, but he seemed to know what that room meant, as he ushered me not unkindly out of the library. After that incident, Henry decided that it was time for us to leave and return to Innsmouth. He took me to the inn to quickly pack up what I had brought and hailed us a cab back to that sodden, muddy burg. On the drive back, he spoke to me quietly but firmly, informing me that I would not be allowed back on campus for a while. For my own sake, of course. He had been told of my wanderings and saw great danger for me there. The further I could get from that room and the books therein, the more stable I would be.

I tell you true, my heart. The idea that I could be unstable - me! Titus Boddicker! - was ludicrous to even put to conception. I have never been more grounded or steadier in my life. I have grown a backbone to stand strong with your parents and their incessant meddling. Their poking and prodding. Their snide little jabs at my profession. They know that being employed in that den of vipers is onerous to me, and yet they insist on mentioning it at every opportunity. They have never thought me good enough for you! Not once have they approved of our marriage! Not once have they said something positive about me! In fact, I would wager all the gold the Weatherbys gave me that they spent the entirety of your time at their home besmirching my character and urging you to leave me behind to marry someone more your status! Well, I will not have it! Do you hear me, Luisa! I will not-

January 27th, 1922

My darling Luisa,

Apologies, my love. I do not know what came over me. A hot flood of anger erupted into my heart, and I cannot tell you for the life of me from whence it originated. I truly apologize for what I wrote if I wrote it at all. I have scribbled through it so many times that it is incomprehensible even to me. The idea that I could be aggressive toward you is beyond what I could imagine. I love your parents. I love the support they have given us as we navigate our early years of marriage. We could not have stayed afloat without them. But this is not important to write, I don't believe. Of more importance is to explain what happened when Henry and I arrived back in Innsmouth and met with Harvey and the EoD.

We stopped off at the manor for me to deposit my things - an instance I shall detail momentarily. Actually, my love, I should speak of it now so as not to worry you. When I arrived at the manor, I was met at the door by Amleragh. You recall Harvey's daughter. She smiled quite prettily and invited me in. For the first time I heard her voice. It was fascinating. Smooth and velvety, yes, but with a faint bubbling sound in her throat. Almost as if she was gargling water in a way, though the idea of such is foolish. She told me as we walked to my chamber that her father was at the temple waiting for us whenever we arrived and that there was no specific rush but that tarrying would not be preferable either. In my own time, she said, and left me to my clothes with a gentle brush of her fingers across my hand. Within me, something sparked but I quickly staunched the flame. I have eyes only for you, my love, my heart. You are all that I think about in ways appropriate to a gentleman. No other such thoughts are allowed within my mind, I assure you. I would never spend a half-second of my time considering the touch of another woman. Not once. Not ever. Of this, you may be assured.

After I left the manor, Henry had made his way back to the front and was waiting patiently for me. He told me that the mud was not something he had missed but that the temple, thankfully, was only a scant few blocks away. As we walked, he told me that I would likely have some poor dreams tonight but that the distance from the books and the university would do me considerable good. He apologized again for placing me in such a situation, but I saw no reason for him to do so. Even the brief glimpse of the words that I saw had changed my view on the world and that, my love, is something that I shall always appreciate. It is of vital importance for one such as I, brilliant and erudite, to periodically have an epiphany to modify how I see the planet around me. Without change, we are stagnant. Without knowledge, we are blind. Without hope, we are useless. Without love, well, we are simply nothing at all. Would you not agree? Of course you would. I know you.

As promised, the walk to the temple was not far, but was impeded by freshly churned mud making every step an effort. By the time we reached the sandstone building - a curious choice given the ramshackle wood nature of the rest of the town - our legs were tired, and our feet were coated to the ankle with thick, clinging brown-black mud. Still, we had arrived and, nearly as soon as we knocked, the door was opened and we were ushered inside by Harvey, looking for all the world as pleased to be here as he would have been drowning in a pool of his own blood. Both Henry and I apologized for our appearance and attempted to scrape the mud from our feet, but Harvey waved a hand. Mud, he said, was as much of the essence of Innsmouth as the water, the fish, and the townsfolk. They did not stand much on appearance here at the Esoteric Order of Dagon, though they did hold strict to several tenets of behavior. Allowing the two of us inside not only to see the temple but read one of their sacred artifacts was, to put it mildly, a large breach of tradition and he hoped that we appreciated the gesture he was making. We both assured him that we did and waited for him to lead the way in his own time. The last thing either of us wanted to do was make him feel more put-out than he clearly already was experiencing.

The temple itself was odd, although I admit that using such a descriptor after all I have experienced already seems slightly overwrought, so to speak. Rather than a warm, welcoming place like I expected, the atmosphere was cold and damp. Not much different from outside, really. In fact, I would dare say that the moisture in the temple was somehow more cloying and stinging than that outside. The rooms were lit with torches, not electricity, and the sandstone from the exterior had been exchanged for a black, slick stone that appeared to be weeping wetness. No sign of a chair or a table or even a rug of any kind appeared as far as I could see. The effect altogether felt unpleasant, like a tomb in a way, and it was glaringly evident that this was not a place for out-of-towners like Henry or myself. This was a haven for those born and bred in Innsmouth and our intrusion was not welcome. Why Harvey had agreed to let us examine one of their texts is beyond me. I did not think I had been especially articulate, though I admit my natural charisma could have charmed his heart. Still, the why was irrelevant, all things considered. He had given us access and we were grateful.

He told us to follow him exactly and we did so, making sure to mirror his movements to the letter. We did not want to trespass more than we had and certainly had no intention of transgressing upon their space. Harvey led us through hallways so dark and winding that I soon lost my bearings and

96

resolved to do nothing more than follow our guide. Some of the corridors were tighter than others, with heavy-looking iron doors placed haphazardly. I bit my tongue to prevent outward judgment of mine from leaking out of my mouth. I could not stop my mind from speaking the critiques, however. Simply put, my darling, the inner workings of the EoD temple felt uncomfortably similar to that of an abandoned prison. Not that I have much experience with the penal system, mind you! But I've had family members - not close, do not fret - be consigned to incarceration and, as we played the role of dutiful loved ones, we would occasionally visit to bring them small treats or news of the outside world. Every time we went, I would stay close to my mother, holding onto her dress. I could feel the eyes of prisoners upon us, and their gaze cut through me. I found out later from my sister that they were not staring at me. Rather, my mother's appearance would bring attention from all those residing in the prison. She was a beautiful woman, as you know, and my father - through tall and strong - posed no intimidation to the convicts. Aside from the feel of predation lurking within the complex, the air was always stale, thick, heavy, and smelt strongly of humanity in all the worst ways. The walls were drab, gray, and cold, and I could not comprehend why someone would voluntarily choose to spend their lives in such an uncomfortable place. When told that they did not do so voluntarily, I was rightfully embarrassed and committed myself to a life of virtue and gentility. However, while the temple was surely a location where those attending chose to congregate, the same feeling of confusion stirred within my breast.

Fortunately, I had been so lost in my thoughts that I had not done anything beyond follow so, when my feet stopped moving, we had arrived. Harvey ushered us into a small room and, similarly to that area in the university, shut and locked the door behind us. If possible, where we now stood was even less welcoming than the rest of the temple. The walls were tight and bare, save a small bookshelf and only a short, thin table in the middle of the floor decorated the chamber. Harvey told us that we were to say nothing while in this holy space and that we would be permitted ten minutes with the requested book. He would be in here the entire time and, if at any point he felt we were being disrespectful, he would call the meeting concluded, remove the book from our presence, and remove us from the temple. This speech was given to us without anger or malice, but Harvey was certainly firm. He also did not retrieve the tome until we both had nodded our assent to the requirements. Satisfied, or apparently so, he reached for the bookshelf and drew from it a sand-colored and well-worn book that he placed on the table. He told us that this book - *The Strictures of Mother Hydra and Father Dagon* - was an integral, indeed indispensable, part of the practices of the EoD and warned us that we were to keep all we saw and read to ourselves. After once again agreeing to his demand, Henry opened the book and began to read. His mouth fell open and I could see terror grip his eyes. He pointed at a passage and told me to read. I did so and what I saw -

January 27th, 1922

My darling Luisa,

[Editor's note: This part of the letter had gotten wet and the ink had run. I was unable to decipher any words beyond what follows.]

--awful id-- rituals involving ---- *fish* --- gold in exc-- village --- three oath--- statues *everywhere*! God, the hor--- this town --- makes sense --- Weatherby. Oh no! The po-- call some---

- and I swear that I will return to you as soon as I can, my darling. I cannot stay in this place. Not with what I know. We were ushered out of the building quickly after our expressions told our stories and Harvey warned us to keep our promises, though he did not threaten my lodging at his manor. I found that quite curiously kind in the wake of what I had just read. My dove, you must destroy this letter once you receive it. You cannot put yourself - or me! - in danger from anything that may come to find this information and snuff it out. My God, the horror. Luisa, I love you more than anything in this world and I know that now. Please, if you value anything of our life together, you wil----

Your-- ing ------ Titus

January 30th, 1922

My dear Luisa,

I dreamed last night. I have been dreaming every night since I left Arkham. My dreams are always the same. Always repeated over and over, unceasingly. It starts with me standing on a long, endless black plain. No grass. No flowers. Nothing but an ever-spreading mass of darkness. I begin to walk and the world spins around me. The sky turns from dark to light and back again. Days pass in the blink of an eye, yet I continue to walk. In my head, inside the dream, words echo. Names. Places, perhaps. *K'Dath. Carcosa*. Names that I cannot bring myself to even put down in ink for fear of inflicting something wicked upon the world. I walk. I walk. I walk. I walk. And nothing changes.

There is a flash of light - blinding, shimmering, painful - and in front of my eyes is a sigil. A symbol. It is ancient and bloody. It is crumbling and newly forged. Spires protrude from it as the color bleeds into it, staining the material a bright, unyielding yellow. Like that of gold, but more so. A Platonic ideal of yellow, perhaps, my love. Something inside the color is sickly and hateful. It speaks to me, blasphemy ringing in my ears, pouring dark cruelty into my mind. Saturating me with it. Taunting me with a future I wish desperately to avoid. I see a hand extend from the sigil. It is long and black and clawed with tattered yellow rags dangling from what must surely be the wrist. The claws grasp the sky and rend it open, pulling the night apart and exposing time beyond time. I see something nameless, shapeless there. Whirling dervishes dance around it as it writhes quietly. Trumpets ring and flutes play and drums thunder out a melody both sweet and discomfiting. It sleeps. I do not know why or how I know such things, but it sleeps. Mercifully, it sleeps. It slumbers and waits and when it awakens, we shall all become no more. The sigil flashes and draws my attention back to it. On top of it, a figure gaunt and spindly, sits and gazes upon me. I cannot see its face, but the entirety of itself is covered in those yellow rags. Perched on a skull elongated and sharp is a crown. Dented. Bent. What jewels once may have been there have been removed and tossed into the void surrounding us. The creature reaches out a hand for me to kiss, a monarch in marigold in front of me, and I kneel. I feel my heart seize, but I kneel just the same. It floats down. God, it floats! It lands in front of me and places the gnarled claws on my shoulder. It is tender in a way such that I cannot describe. The tyrant bids me look at it and, before I do, I wake up.

Luisa, in my dream, I want nothing more than to look at the face of this creature, but my mind remains tethered to this world of ours. To you. To the heart you create within me. You save me from losing myself, as silly as that sounds. You have saved me.

I know that I have not returned to you yet. I have tried. Again and again, I have searched for a way to reach the train station, but something prevents me from doing so. A particularly heavy deluge of rain. Slick, sticky mud that is impossible to traverse. Lights that flash and I lose time. I fought these signs for days, it feels like, but once I accepted that I still have a job to complete here in town, they seemed to disappear. The town of Innsmouth returned to whatever passes for normal in this damned place and now I am trapped here until I finish my calling. When that will be, I do not know. I wish that I could explain to you the depth of how I miss you. How I ache for your arms around me, holding me and shielding me from the ravages of this world around us. Luisa, you are my anchor to the idea of joy. I have not been what you deserve, but you will have all of what you can take from me once I make it home to you. It will be soon. It must be. ~~For now, I am haunted and~~ -

January ~~27ᵗʰ32nd~~ *30th, 1922*

My darling Luisa,

Greetings, my love! I hope you are having pleasant weather! I have only recently returned to Innsmouth from Arkham and, I must say, it is strangely refreshing to be back in such a small, quaint place as this. Perhaps it was an overindulgence in the food and sightseeing in Arkham, but the relative peace and quiet of the little town feels quite comforting. I believe that Henry and I will be meeting with Harvey this evening to peruse the book he promised we could see. How exciting! Wait, is that tonight? I am unsure. I have not been sleeping well, I am afraid, my love. I would put it down to the fish and wine that make up the majority of the meals here. Not that I do not enjoy both in great quantities, but they certainly must affect one's digestion, yes? Are your parents taking care of you as I am away? I recall from your last letter that you were feeling poorly. I'm afraid that I will be unable to return to you quite yet, as I still must look into the affairs of young Weatherby, but I have no doubt that such an endeavor will be of no consequence to a mind such as mine! I shall do my utmost to complete the examination and come back to you as soon as possible.

Did I tell you of the contract I have been perusing with Harvey? I must have, surely. It is quite fascinating! There is some sort of compact between the town of Innsmouth and another town, I believe, called Dagon. Or is it Depones? Is that how it is pronounced? Forgive me, dove. I am merely speaking aloud through the ink I sent to you in torrents. You must get frightfully bored of my missives, though I know with certainty that you would never tell me so even if it were the reality! You are far too kind and genteel to break my spirit in such a way! My darling, I miss you desperately. I miss your kisses on my ear and your hand clasped tenderly in mine. I miss our sunset walks and the morning skies pink with promise as we wake up together. I miss our meals together, fancy or simple. I miss the crocheted blanket on our bed that your grandmother passed down to you upon her untimely passing. I miss our evenings at home. I miss our afternoons out at the plays. I miss everything about you. I hope that I should return to you soon.

January 30th, 1922

My darling Luisa,

Christ, what am I saying? What was that? None of that will ever be the same. None of that has ever *been*. We have had lovely experiences, but we have had difficult times, I know. The fish here are rotted to the core, just like this town and any attempt of mine to pretend otherwise would be

January 30th, 1922

My darling Luisa,

    A darn lie, since there is no proof of the corruption in this town! I cannot imagine that anyone could treat this place as anything other than quaint. Young Weatherby must surely be on a trip with some young beauty he found around town. The ladies of Innsmouth are intriguing in a handsome way, though I of course have eyes for none but you. Though, I must be honest when I tell you that Harvey's daughter, Amleragh, is quite comely and has been intimating through shy glances and gentle touches on my arm that she wishes for a relationship beyond basic courteous cordiality. I would never do so, love! ~~You are the only one for me. I cannot lie to you, though, and tell you that I am being ignored for I am not. It is a test, my angel, and I intend to complete~~

January 30th, 1922

My darling Luisa,

My mind is foggy, my darling. The fog I saw -
I *know* I saw - around Henry's face has somehow
reached from Arkham into my mind and swirled
around the meat inside. I feel as if in a daze at
times. As if the world is not entirely real around me.
It is ridiculous, I know. But do not believe the
honeyed words I write about this town. There is
something deep underneath this land that worries
me to my heart. I do not know exactly what ~~yes I
do~~

January 30th, 1922

My darling Luisa,

~~I do know what lurks here. Love, love beyond that which humanity could ever share with one another. Love that stretches out into the cosmos with long, languid ropes.~~

January 30th, 1922

My darling Luisa,

The books. The books, Luisa. I must rest. I must sleep. I think I shall drink myself unconscious to stem the flow of what comes to my mind.

Wait for me, my love. Freedom will come soon, in one way or another.

Your loving Titus

February 2nd, 1922

My sweet Luisa,

I have not fallen into darkness or despair. Worry yourself not! The meetings I have recently had with Harvey and Henry have been productive beyond what I could have imagined. Henry appeared satisfied with having read the book and taken a few notes, all of which were of course approved by Harvey. He was grateful for my assistance, and I found no small gratification in having helped facilitate something that spreads knowledge. He told me that he will shortly return to Miskatonic and attempt to find a link between the nonsense written in the EoD's book and whatever may lurk within the tomes held fast in that locked room. Perhaps then, he said, whatever dark thoughts may be plaguing me will flee. I found that strange, as I spoke to none about the dreams of mine. None, save you, my love. In the interest of fairness, I am unfortunately confident that my appearance over the last couple of weeks has degraded in an unacceptable way. I have a slight bit of stubble if you can believe that! I should shave presently. There is something so unseemly about a man in the throes of his hair growing. Clean-shaven or bearded, I say! There is no middle ground.

That is something of this town that strikes me of peculiar, though you could as easily throw a pebble and strike mud here as find something queer and confusing. An exceeding few of the men in town maintain any sort of facial decoration! Harvey has a bushy black beard, yes, and one or two of the other men who may comprise what one could call the 'higher society' of Innsmouth also have a beard, mustache, or something similar. The rank and file, though, have no such adornments on their sallow, thin faces. One wonders if such growth were even possible, given their genetics! That sounds unkind and ungenerous of me, my love, so I apologize. I do so try not to judge, but becoming reacclimated to Innsmouth has brought such curiosity to my mind. The sheer, unbridled ugliness of the residents at times befuddles me. It is as if they are not entirely human, which is absurd.

Is it? I recall something from the book at the temple. What was that again? I forget, I am afraid. My sleep has been fitful and my mind is unclear at times. A far cry from your sharp-witted Titus, eh what? You recall the rapier cleverness with which I have skewered many of my contemporaries who dared make advances on you. How dare they? To assume that I would not fight for that which is mine? Pfah! The arrogance! Ah, yes. That reminds me. Have you contacted the Weatherbys yet? I have made no progress on their case and I begin to find myself feeling slightly guilty for taking their pay without having delivered what they contracted. I am sure the son is here somewhere. I have seen him! At least, I believe I have. No, no. I am sure that I have. For the life of me, I cannot recall where, though. Blame it on the fine wine here, I suppose? I am no drunkard, my love, so you may relax. I have limited myself to one glass per night and have certainly not fallen into drunkenness or a stupor like some sort of common lout. I have too much pride for that!

I must say, though, that there is a sense of unease that has settled over the town. No, not unease. Something else. Nervousness? Excitement? I am unsure of what specifically has changed, but it is evident in the way the townsfolk move and speak. The way they drink and converse. Some appear nigh on jubilant while others trudge around morosely. It is perplexing and not something that I find altogether comforting. I have asked those few townsfolk I have built a fragile kinship with about the goings-on but have been met with nothing but stony stares from blank eyes. Even those that seemed delighted would not say a single word until I changed the subject to something else. The fishing, for example, is a particular favorite of the dockworkers and they could speak for days on the subject. They lament the burdock disappearing but seem optimistic that the whitefish, whichever species that may be, will return soon and favor the town with a renewal of fortune. Why I tell you this, I do not know. I have resorted to eavesdropping on conversations - yes, I know how filthy a habit it is - in order to get some sort of idea of what may be occurring. There are whispers of a festival coming to town, though I do not know what self-respecting circus would attempt to set up shop in such a muddy, dire town. Still, they speak of Innsmouth regaining the prestige it once held. They speak of gold and fish returning to their nets. They talk in hushed, glowing tones of the brilliant outsider who corrected the compact to renew a relationship long since fractured. Despite their lack of awareness of my presence, I found myself quite flattered. Brilliance, indeed! I simply helped find verbiage to better clarify this nebulous deal which had not been enforced in recent years. I do not know what happened to separate Innsmouth from this town of Dagon but -

No. No, Dagon is not a town. I remember that now. It is not a community. It is...something. A thing. A thing? It is as if there has been a lock placed on my memories. I cannot think of exactly what it may refer to, but I *know* that Dagon is nothing so innocuous as a village with a long-running feud. No. Not at all. Dagon is something *other than*. It is something that is not. I can see what it is not, yes. Yes, my love, I know with great certainty what Dagon is not. I simply cannot identify or clarify what it *is* and something in that troubles me. Does it not trouble you? Does it not strike fear in your breast? Your perfect breast? With a beating heart beneath, pumping your blue blood throughout your body? No, Luisa, Dagon is and has been and will be again, but what that means escapes me. That makes no sense. It cannot. Does it not? God, the thinking is clouded. So dark and misty. When I think of something else, the fog clears right as rain. My mental acuity is sharper than it ever has been, to tell the truth. Sums and words come to my mind unbidden, and I find a sense of elocution beyond even what I previously possessed. As you know, that is no mean feat as my wit was legendary in town. Something has brought a spark to my abilities, and I find that to be addictive in a way akin to that of an opium addict, yet without the harm to the mind or body. Does that make sense, my love? I am unsure what exactly I mean by all of this.

Darling, something is happening here that I do not understand. Something beyond the comprehension of anyone here on Earth. I do not want you to come visit me. I do not want you to see how I am doing. I want you to live your life. I miss you terribly, more than words are capable of expressing tenfold, but I feel as if I am being inextricably drawn into something that I cannot escape. I am like a fish caught in a net. I have not been dragged ashore and consumed by violence yet, but the water churns around me, white foam rising to the surface. I feel others here next to me. Some understand our peril. Others do not. Still others embrace it. Something in Innsmouth is broken, my love, and a sinking feeling in the very depth of me believes that I shall soon be broken along with it.

I love you dearly. I wish to see you again. I want to. I need to. But I cannot put you in danger. My mind and heart in combat once more! Damn this place. Damn this world.

Hold on, my heart.

Your devoted Titus

February 4th, 1922

My beautiful Luisa,

You must forgive me my hyperbole in previous letters. A combination of loneliness, feeling other, and an omnipresent dampness will take their toll on a man's mind, let me assure you. I find that I have become annoyingly hysterical at times, jumping at shadows like some cowardly kitten. Innsmouth is a town. A dirty, muddy, unfriendly town. But that is all that it is. There is nothing dark or untoward here. A good night's sleep reminded me of that.

Yes, my dear, all it took was a restful night at the manor and I feel much better now than I have in days prior. The dreams, while still unsettling, have subsided in intensity to the point that I only recall them in vague discomfort rather than active horror. The company has helped me as well. Henry did return to Arkham to do whatever he will be doing with the information he found, but I have spent significant time with Harvey and his charming daughter Amleragh. We have sat in his parlor and consumed fine tea - actual tea, not some mishmash of dirt and weeds found in Innsmouth - and brandy and have spoken at length about events in town and out of town. Amleragh, that otherworldly beauty, was quite keen to learn about my life with you in our town. She was left enraptured by the most tiresome and mundane tasks that I have had to perform in my duties as the solicitor. I must say, it was refreshing to see such curiosity in the eyes of someone. Not that your eyes are not the pinnacle of beauty, of course, darling, but such admiration has been missing in my life for quite some time. Do not take this as criticism! I am simply stating a concern that has been in my heart for months now. I am not impressive to you. I do not make you swoon. Not anymore. I am aware that such a reduction in passion is common for long-term relationships and marriages and have been prepared to navigate those waters, but I will not lie to you. It damages my sense of self every time you yawn or roll your eyes when I speak of that which intrigues me. Your flat affect when you respond to my frustration with my job does nothing to assuage my worries. With Amleragh, though, she is interested in *everything* I have to say! You are still my love and my life, but such attention being paid to me is flattering and I will not say otherwise.

However, I must say the weather has gotten considerably worse as of late as well. Whereas I had become somewhat accustomed to the dampness and chill in the air and the mud that turned the roads into hazards, there has been what I would call a significant increase in moisture in Innsmouth. Rain comes down frequently now, cold and icy, and it cuts to the very marrow of one's bones, even after a scant few minutes outdoors. I have taken to bringing another shirt and tie along with me wherever I go so that I may change into something fresh and dry upon my arrival. As always, though, I am unique in town for doing so. The rest of the residents of this place seem perfectly content to walk around in the rain without an issue. In fact, I have seen more smiles after this weather has begun than in times prior to now. Perhaps they like the wetness? This is an odd town, my darling, but you know this exceedingly well by now.

Fortunately, with the contentedness of the townsfolk, they have lowered their guard around me. I would not categorize them as 'friendly', as I do not believe that such behavior is even possible within this place, but they have certainly been less aggressively antagonistic. Indeed, one or two of the more outgoing (for what that is worth here) townsfolk saw fit to purchase me a glass of wine and ask me to sit with them last night. Initially, I was concerned - as would anybody be - but they assured me they meant no harm and, rather, wanted to speak to me to obtain my insight into the contract upon which I worked. Word of it must have been spread around town and the two men (again, such as it is) were quite keen to understand what I thought of the contract and when I believed they may see the recommencement of the terms. I was honest with the gentlemen in telling them that I was not sure, but that surely the town of Dagon would be more than willing to work with Innsmouth. For some reason, that drew a laugh from them. A dark, guttural, choking laugh that was less full of joy than a strange sort of amusement at my expense. I must have said something wrong, for they continued to chide me for my misunderstanding.

Yes, that's right. Dagon! I had forgotten. God, I forget more and more these days. Dagon is not a town. I must remember that. I must commit that to memory deep in my mind. The two of them explained that Dagon is not a town. It is not a town. *Not* a town. It is something more. Bigger. A city? No. Not in such terms. Something more like an idea. Is Dagon an idea? I recall asking them and they told me that I was half-right. Which half? I asked and they laughed again. I do not think I enjoy the sound of their laughter all that much, Luisa. It hurts me in a way I dare not explicate. It is a harshness, like sandpaper on my soul. Is that right? ~~Do I know? Do I know anything anymore? I can't~~

The weather here, my love, has gotten worse. Rain upon rain upon rain. Did I say that already? I cannot read my own handwriting sometimes. I fear that my vision may be going, but there is this fog that fills my eyes sometimes. I hope it is just dampness that will leave when I do so. I do not know for sure, though, when that will be. When I leave, I need to take something with me. What was it? Why was I here again? Surely you remember, love!

120

Right! Lucien. Yes. Yes. The Weatherby boy. I asked Harvey about him point-blank yesterday. I think. I asked where he was. Some little part of my humanity cannot give up on him. Could not. Cannot. Harvey was the same as always, but he did confirm the lad is in town. He said that he was safe and being cared for. That he had an invitation to the festival and, oh, by the way, would I like to attend as well? I am not entirely sure that the 'invitation' is something that I will be allowed to refuse. Not that I feel threatened, mind you. I am, in reality, quite intrigued by ~~the young Miss Marsh~~ the festivities, but there is no doubt lurking anywhere within this vast mind of mind that those who inhabit this town would quite easily fall to violence and feel little to no remorse in meting it out on those they deem worthy of experiencing it. That means, then, that I will be here for the foreseeable future, as they have not told me specifically when the festival is or what exactly it entails. I hope for something gentle and pleasant, but seeing as nothing in this town particularly embodies either quality, my expectations are lower than I would prefer.

All the same, I am pleased that I have reached a point where I am tolerated by this community. I see their hard work in the background of the world now. They scrape and scrounge to find food and employment. Whereas my opinion of the town is still quite critical, I cannot feel contempt for these simple folk. Nor can I necessarily feel pity for them, strange as that may sound. They live a hard life, a life far more strenuous than I wish for myself or any of those that I love, but it is not a bad life, as it is. It is just...life.

Oh! Before I forget, as I am wont to do these days, I must tell you of what I found in Harvey's library. The other day - I cannot remember which - I was feeling poorly and opted to stay inside and allow myself to relax and heal up. At the very least, it kept me from the damp for a day. Well, slumber may only hold a man's attention for so long before he longs for some kind of activity. Harvey had gone out to conduct business and, while I did not know where Amleragh was, I did not fear her surprising me. Feeling emboldened, I made my way to Harvey's library and sneaked inside with as little noise as I could muster. Once inside, I shut the door silently behind me and slowly turned the lock to prevent any other unwanted visitors from entering. It was then I allowed myself to breathe and peruse the shelves. I had obtained a slight idea of what the library held within it on previous visits, but I had always been interrupted by someone or another preventing me from looking further. Now, though, I was free to snoop as I wished. In the interest of true honesty, very little of the library was unexpected. Books on travel and fishing. Large dictionaries and thesauruses. Thick, dry books on the practice of law. Then, I saw it.

I could scarce believe my eyes. Tucked into the back of one of the lower shelves near the back of the room, I saw the telltale dark coloration of a book spine that brought back memories from Miskatonic. I found it difficult to envision a world in which Harvey would allow such a book to sit, ignored, in his library where anyone could find it. Certainly not where Amleragh could get herself into trouble! He would never put her in danger, even inadvertently. Still, I found it incumbent upon me to check and assuage my concerns about the book.

With a trembling hand, I reached over and pulled the book from the shelf. It was pushed in quite deeply and required a steady tug. Once I had it in my hands, however, I could tell straight away that it was not the same book, at least not of the same veracity. The cover was threadbare and worn with a clearly bovine leather strap around it. The lettering on the front was clear and distinct, with *Necronomicon* printed in big, bold, black letters. The pages were cream-colored and appeared to be in reputable condition. I knew that it was not the same book, though, because I did not feel it in my soul. I did not feel the pull of something deep within me and outside of me. I did not feel the urge to open the book, at least not more than usual when it comes to new books. When I *did* open it, nothing sprang into my mind. Nothing pulled me elsewhere. There were words. Nothing but words. Confusing words, yes. Words of ominous portent, certainly.

But nothing more than that. Some of the phrases I recognized. I had seen them before, though where I could not tell you. Names, perhaps, but a mishmash of consonants and vowels in unpronounceable smears of letters. ***Yog-Sothoth. Cthulhu. Iä! Cthulhu fhtagn! Ph'nglui mglw'nfah Cthulhu R'lyeh wgah'nagl fhtagn!***

Wait. Oh no. Oh Christ. I wrote that phrase to you before, did I not? Something about it being German? I exposed you to it! What have I *done*? Luisa, you must read this with a clear mind and do exactly as I say. Burn all other letters I have sent you before burning this one. Put them all to the flame and then burn the ashes once more. And then burn this one in similar fashion. Take the ashes of all these letters, place them in a container such as a vase, seal it entirely with wax, pack that away into a trunk, then take the trunk to the ocean as far out as you can manage, dump it into the black depths of the sea, and pray that whatever mental infection has reached into my life has not reached yours. Burn every letter from me you receive as well. I must keep you safe. Luisa, my love, I cannot forgive myself for having left you vulnerable to this book, these words. How could I ever have thought that such a book would be innocuous, even if it were not of the same quality as the true book at the university? Foolish. I have been foolish. You could not have known.

Luisa, I want to be home with you. I say this often, but it rings true on every occasion. I feel nothing but worry and contempt for this town.

I need to save you so you may save me.

I love you deeply.

Your tired Titus

February 4th, 1922

My Luisa,

I see Lucien wherever I look. He is there and he is
not there. Was he a lure? A trap? Is he here or am I
dreaming it all?

I know not, love.
I know not love.

T

February 8th, 1922

My Luisa,

I have failed you. No, not regarding those damned words I sent to you, though my heart is pained by that mistake as well. No, my darling, I am sick to death that I have betrayed you. Betrayed us. Betrayed the sanctity of our life together. I have no excuse, no reason. I cannot explain my actions away. All I can do is prostrate myself before you, at least in words, and hope beyond hope that you may find forgiveness in that wide, deep heart of yours for such a wretched beast as I. You deserve the truth and an explanation, though it will hurt you to read as much as I hurt writing it. But there must be no secrets between us, so this is part of my penance.

I gave in to temptation. Yes, with Amleragh. I imagine you may have surmised as much through past letters, though I swear on the graves of my family members that nothing untoward had occurred before last night. It had been a long day. The weather continues to pour rain and turn the streets into rivers of filthy water and mud. I did not feel up to exiting the manor, as a slight cold had taken hold of my head, and I told Harvey to go about his business without me. He hardly needs me to aid him anymore and, between the two of us, I think he may simply keep me around as a curiosity or out of pity. Perhaps both. We shall see how long that endures, however, given the events of yesterday. I apologize, I will continue. As I said, Harvey went out to manage whatever business he is involved with these days and Amleragh told him that we would find ways of entertaining ourselves in the manor. Looking back on her words, I should not have been surprised by her actions later, but the girl and her father exchanged a look before he left. I have spent some time considering what that mental exchange meant, but I can arrive at no satisfactory conclusion. I don't believe that he would have placed his daughter in a position where a mongrel such as I could take advantage of her, but I simply cannot be sure. Regardless, he left and then the girl and I were alone together.

By this point, the two of us had managed to strike up a collegiality, if not outright friendship, that allowed us to speak freely and engage each other in games of the mind and intellect. Despite her age, she is brilliant in the ways of the world and hardly sheltered in her outlook. She is shockingly cosmopolitan in her views and has made it clear on many occasions that she longs to experience a larger city than this burg. We had fallen into a pattern of chatting for a while after a meal, sharing stories - mainly her listening to my tales about the cities outside Innsmouth - and enjoying each other's company before adjourning to the library for a match or two of chess. Did I not mention Harvey's chess set, my darling? Of course! Yes, he has the most uniquely beautiful set I have ever placed my eyes upon. The board itself is a cloudy crystal with real onyx and mother-of-pearl as the squares. The pieces are of gold and silver, but they are surely merely coated with the precious metal. The two armies, as it were, are the most fascinating aspect of the board, however. On one side, the white side, the army is made of human-like figures carved out of ivory. Each of the figures is meticulously detailed in a strangely modern fashion, such as policemen rather than knights and peasants instead of pawns. The other side, in contrast, is far different. The pieces are obsidian and sharp but are grotesque in form, resembling fish-like monsters with grasping hands. The queen is a tall, imposing figure with a shrouded aspect. The king, though, is the most bizarre. It is fat and bulbous with small bat-like wings protruding from its back and long, sucking tentacles attached to its mouth like some sort of squid. If I am being honest, as I must from every point here until the end of time, the king is uncomfortable to gaze upon. It as if some malign presence inhabits the very stone of the piece, waiting to be used. The queen is not quite as discomfiting, but it is still unpleasant to spend much time observing. Naturally, I allow Amleragh to use the black side every time, as she seems to feel more kinship with those pieces and I simply want as little to do with the royalty of the black as necessary.

The first game yesterday was standard as it always has been. We talked idly as we played. She would make an aggressive play and I would block it before countering with one of my own. Now, I am not what one would call advanced in my skills at chess, but I believe I can hold my own with any who come across my path. Any, that is, save Amleragh. Surely, she must have competed in tournaments in the past, for she is nigh on unbeatable. The strategies she uses are counter-intuitive and bizarre, but they seem to work to perfection. Any attempt I have made to learn the move structures she utilizes does nothing but provide an itch to my poor brain. It does not particularly matter, of course. I am not speaking about her proficiency in chess because you do not care about such. No, you need to know what occurred between the two of us. I shall arrive there presently. It was during the second game wherein the basic pleasantries changed direction to something more...intimate. She asked me about you and how long we had been together. I told her of our life together and how we had met. I told her of our chance meeting at Castronelli's Bistro. How you had spilled a full plate of Bolognese on me as a waitress, but I was so smitten with your eyes that I did not feel the heat from the fresh dish. How we went on our first date on a walk through the park and how the dappled sun landed on you and made you appear as if an angel. I spoke of our quiet nights and busy days, our meals and our arguments and our jokes. I spoke of your touch in the middle of the night when you think I am asleep and cannot feel you caressing my face.

It was at that moment that she stood up and walked over to me. I could feel my heart hitch a beat as she approached me and asked if your touch felt like 'this' before running her hand over my cheek. Her hand was soft and smooth and cool and the daintiness in her fingers belied the strength in her arms. I should have told her to remove her hand. That it was inappropriate. That her father would be furious. That I was married - or whatever we are - and that I could not indulge in whatever desires I wished. I should have told her a thousand things in a thousand different ways and a thousand different languages, but I did not. My breath caught in my throat and electricity raced down to my toes and back up my body like countless spiders searching for a home. The air in my lungs fell heavy and my mouth grew dry. My hands grasped the arms of the chair and the hard, unyielding wood felt like a life preserver in the middle of her ocean. I admitted the truth, much as it pained me inside. The truth was and is that at your touch did not and does not feel like that. Your touch, gentle and warm, is no less important to me than the breath in my lungs, but it was not the same as hers. In her touch - the mere touch of her hand! - was youth and a strange kind of life beyond that I could imagine within you. You have age and wisdom in your hands. You have a confidence and tenderness born from years of comfort and familiarity. Your touch is that of reminding. Hers was not that. Hers was newness, freshness. Hers was energy and exploration. Hers crackled with the excitement of uncertainty. It infused my soul with something like water to a man lost in the desert, though that comparison is too crass. I felt in her caress a sense of aching desire that has long since dissipated in our love in favor of affectionate sameness. It was not better - it was different.

She looked at me then and I could see the actual beauty in her. There was an exoticness to her that I still cannot place. Her wide, pouting, shy mouth. Her large, blue-green eyes no different than the ocean lapping at the shore. Her hair fell to her shoulders in a cloud of ebony. She does not compare to you, my sweet, in any way that is important. You outshine her like the sun does a candle in the middle of the day. In that moment, though, beauty did not matter as it should. Something about her presence spoke to something within me. Something primal that desires nothing more than to indulge the basest of instincts. I shivered and she moved her hand to my hair, running her fingers across my scalp. Her nails felt like claws scraping my skin, but ripples burst in my chest from excitement. She asked if it was okay that she touch me and I told her yes. I do not have any reason or excuse other than I had no ability to refuse her in that moment. She sat in my lap then, shifting her skirt so that her legs could drape over mine. I saw the skin of her legs, creamy but with a shimmer to them, and felt her drape her other hand over my shoulder. She was unavoidable now, sitting where she was, and she stroked the back of my neck with her fingers. I still felt no heat from her, but wave after wave of heat poured from me to warm the both of us. She did not smirk, as one might expect from a woman who had achieved her goal, but instead looked at me with a calm, gentle smile that pulled honeyed words from my mouth. I do not remember what I said. I do not even recall if the words were English. Were I not so consumed with my guilt, I would examine the words more closely in my mind. I cannot say that *Dagon* was one of the words. Not definitively. Yet, I cannot positively ensure that it was not.

Regardless, I spoke sweetly to her, words that must have been what she wanted to hear, because she leaned forward and kissed me then. As with the rest of her, her lips were cool and soft and promised greater pleasures ahead. I recall distinctly that my hands nigh on snapped the arms of the chair as the last vestiges of restraint held onto me with a grip like that of death. When she took that hand of hers, though...that soft, sweet hand...and placed it on my leg, I had nothing left within me to resist. I shall spare you the gruesome details, my love. I do not wish to inflict further pain upon you. I will say,

133

though, that my mind and body did not feel my own as we engaged in congress. My arms and hands moved of their own accord and her bucking hips seemed to latch around me with desperation. When finally we completed our encounter, as it were, she left quickly and my mind clearly immediately. Like fog blown away by a strong breeze, my faculties had returned to me and the weight of what had occurred landed on me with full force. I cannot express how pained I am for what happened. It matters not how I felt or the control that I had. I have betrayed you and my soul is heavy with regret. My love, I would never wish to cause you more agony than you have right now. My only prayer is that you have done as I requested in my previous missive and have burned this letter without reading it. I will spend the rest of my days in submission to you, searching with a singular purpose for a way to simply begin to make up for my transgressions. My angel, this place has damned us all. I fear the rain will wash me away with it and, for now, I welcome such a result. I will not dignify such intrusive thoughts as a permanent end to my existence, but I must leave Innsmouth at the next opportunity. If I do not, I may never leave.

I love you.

Your Titus

February 12th, 1922

My dear Luisa,

You have not written back for a while. I suppose I should not have expected differently. After what I did to you, I cannot be forgiven. In fact, I am not sure why I continue to write to you. I cannot envision a world in which you wish to speak to me once more. I suppose that now I write because it is what I have become accustomed to doing in my free moments. A habit or a tradition, if you will, that tethers me still to the outside world. You may feel free to discard these missives upon receiving them if you so wish. I just do not feel...right, I suppose, in stopping them. I need to believe that there is a place beyond Innsmouth. Some place that is not Arkham. Some place free from the darkness that washes over this part of the state with a melancholy sort of hatred.

This all sounds so dramatic, I know. It is unlike me to be so hyperbolic or speak of such things, but this town does something to a mind. It makes a man forget who he is. What he believes. What he knows to be real and true. Did I go into that temple days ago? I cannot be sure. It seems like a memory half-forgotten over time. The fog in my mind grows opaquer by the day and I struggle at times to even remember you, though I often wish I could not. What I did is not forgivable, but I have difficulty recalling exactly what happened. It feels like a dream, though I know it was not. Was it? Did I just have a terrible nightmare in which I betrayed you? Certainly it must be possible, yes? I would never choose to do such a thing to you. Yes, it certainly must have been a dream. A dream and nothing more. That should ensure your forgiveness now! It is like a weight being lifted from my heart to know that you will come back to my arms once more now that we have cleared up such a disgusting mess as that dream.

My love, the festival grows near in town. The townsfolk of Innsmouth grow more vibrant in their own way. They talk more in their burbling voices. They move quicker through the mud and drink more peat wine. They laugh, a curious hacking sound, and they appear happy. Even their skin has lost the dishwater dullness that it once had. If my eyes are to be believed, something I do not take for granted any more, they appear to have something of a sheen to them. An iridescence that normally one only sees in fish scales or abalone, but that idea is patently ludicrous. All the same, it is nice to be able to walk around this place without feeling as if I am going to be attacked. I am not welcomed in as a part of their community, but they do not seem to mind my presence. Harvey has also been more gregarious in recent days, speaking of a great revival which will be coming soon. I assume at the festival, but he has not said so with certainty. I have asked what sort of revival he means and the response I have gotten is always a thank you for my help in renewing the contract and that those in town are grateful for my aid. He has assured me that, when Father and Mother return to Innsmouth, I will be one of the first to meet them. Right at the front of the line! I am led to believe that such a place is one of great prominence, which has served to placate me for the time being. I want to be back with you, but I must be here until the festival is over. As soon as it finishes, though, my angel, I shall return to you with bells on. You have my word.

I find myself running out of words to say to you at present. I must see you. Hold you. Touch you. Kiss you. I must slumber next to you and sleep the dreamless sleep of the righteous. Yes, no more dreams. That sounds lovely.

Titus

February 12th, 1922

My Luisa,

My dear, I continue to dream of dark things. The sigil. The king. The sickening yellow. All of that returns again and again, but now they are joined by others. Not friends. No relationship of that sort. Yet, not rivals. Allies, perhaps. It began a day or two ago. The king was there, demanding my fealty, but next to him - it? - was another figure. This one was tall - extremely so - and skinny, nigh to a skeleton. It was blacker than midnight and a coldness resonated from within it. Coldness? Maybe. Somewhat, I think. Something frigid but also hot, warmed through, delighted by flame. Something that flourishes in chaos and destruction. A gleeful stagehand in the worst of humanity. No, not a stagehand. A puppet master, perhaps. No, that does not feel correct either.

Forgive me, love, but I must expel these thoughts and dreams from my mind as if they were poison. Perhaps they are indeed just that. This creature beside the king, though, is not - was not - hungry. Not like the king, he of the endless hunger for Something Else. The beast in black was - is - not as primally focused on consumption. It does not demand fealty and worship, not like the monster in goldenrod. No, it glories in what men may do to one another. Encourages it. Exacerbates it. Turns violent

138

thoughts into bloody reality. It has its hands in war and strife, famine and death. Four Horsemen in the swirl of shadow underneath the cloak. It toys with us, dove. We are its playthings and it does not play kindly or gently. It frightens me more than the king. It knows what it does. It knows what we fear. It knows how to use that fear for itself.

There is more, though, my sweetness. I see Innsmouth in my dreams. I see the town reborn - in the future or the past, I cannot tell - and flourishing with life and joy. The damp is gone, replaced by warm, salty air. The mud no longer cakes the streets as pavement winds like a snake through the town. Gold and fish are piled in crates by the water as sailors arrive with more bounty than I ever would have imagined this town capable of providing. It seems idyllic but something in my heart seizes as I see in the distance two figures watching over the town. Gargantuan, hideous things, staring down impassively as the townsfolk move and live like ants under their gaze. Scaled and dark, tentacled and wet. I know - *I know* - what this is, what they are now. Father and Mother. The parents and the lifeblood of Innsmouth. They had been estranged for only God knows what reason, but now they have reconciled. *I* have reconciled them. I have brought them together to bellow the song that ends the world. They will return at the festival and it is my fault.

Luisa, I cannot bear much more horror. I cannot imagine that I have done so little and yet so much. I cannot envision a world without us together or a world without anyone. I no longer care about finding the Weatherby boy or attending the festival. I only wish to return to you. To redeem myself for the dream I had - if indeed a dream it were - and rededicate myself to you and to us. You are -

Too good for me. Yes, you are too good for me. For this beaten, frightened man writing you. My love turns to ash in my mouth. I am becoming resolved. For love of you, I will ~~not~~ return. I ~~cannot~~ bear it all. The world looms ~~too~~ large ~~for a man such as me. I am drowning.~~

February 12th, 1922

My dear Luisa,

Drowning? Pfah. Ignore my hyperbole. My sleep has been poor as of late, but I intend to remedy that with a good night's rest tonight. I shall be right as rain tomorrow and come to you as soon as the festival ends. I have allowed my mind to wander for far too long now. The ramblings of one tired and ready for excitement. The festival awaits in two days!

You are my love and my life, Luisa.

I shall be with you soon as I possibly can.

Titus

February 13, 1922

My Luisa,

I hope I am writing this in reality. I hope this is a letter you receive from me and read and destroy. I hope that this actually is occurring, but I have lost my ability to determine whether or not that is the case. I continue to dream, love. Night after night, I fear closing my eyes, but exhaustion takes me over as if being swallowed by some gigantic creature and then I am back there. The long, endless, black plain, studded with ruins of cities long since demolished. The sky writhing and bubbling with unholy colors. The king. The dark presence. And something else. Something other than what has come before. Something that wishes to come again. It looms in the background, wings flapping gently, patiently. I see two figures in front of me, their hands joined lovingly, though no force in the universe could call their connection 'love'. It is confusing, I know. I am confused myself. I am confused *about* myself. I want to understand it all, but when I understand it, I cannot speak it. Cannot write it. Cannot explicate it. It is as if understanding and placing the pieces of the puzzle together removes my ability to communicate with you and others. Like a wall is built between their world and ours and I am not allowed to live in both, though I desperately want to - need to - make sense of it. I have seen beyond some veil, angel, and I wish I could show everyone so that I would not be alone.

I feel alone. So alone. Physically, yes, but more than that. Mentally, I am above and below all. Spiritually, I have felt what remains of my soul torn to tatters and dangled in front of me. Taunted by it, as if a hound restrained from raw meat. There is no cruelty in it that I can find. Perhaps there is. Perhaps it is the epitome of cruel and I am simply inured to it by now. Who can tell? All I do know is that my dreams are no longer a safe place for me. That the festival tomorrow shall be the dawning of a new life of sorts. Of a sort? I know not.

You see how language flees from me more frequently now, my sweet? Words, once my greatest weapon against the forces of brainless, shambling masses, have become dulled. I have lost my edge, my sharpness. So, I must return. I must view that damned book once more. I must let the words and visions, profane and beautiful, pour into me and fill up this empty vessel which I have become. I have been hollowed. Hallowed? Both, perhaps. I apologize for my lack of clarity, my heart. My thoughts are clouded with weariness. I have told you of the dreams, yes? Of course I have. I must have. Surely I would not keep that from you.

The dreams, yes.

I love you?

Your Titus

February 13, 1922

My Luisa,

Harvey is excited, more than I have ever seen, as he puts the final touches on the festival tomorrow. He has enlisted much of the community to set up events of some kind on the beach and by the temple. In his busy state, he has not paid attention to my comings and goings, which has allowed me to wander as I choose throughout the day. Nothing in this town is alive, my darling. Sure, there are things living, but nothing is *alive*. Dead, decaying wood, rotting fish, mindless townsfolk. This town has died and nobody will acknowledge it, save to proclaim out of nowhere that the festival shall bring back Innsmouth and renew its faith and its hope. I wish I could be skeptical as I once was, but I find myself compelled by them. I can come up with no words to counterbalance their exuberance. Something will happen. Something *is* coming. And if it is that which will revitalize this cursed place, I fear in my heart of hearts what the cost shall be of such a rebirth.

I have not seen young Weatherby lately, by the by. I have scoured the town in my moments of lucidity, though they be few and far between, and he is nowhere to be found. Wherever he is, they keep him secluded and guarded. How can I know that, my love? Truth be told, I cannot know. I wish I could say for certain, but I believe in some dark part of me that he will be an integral part of this festival in ways that one can hardly imagine. I fear for the poor boy, but what can one such as I do? I am only one man - a wonderful man, yes - but just a singular person. To be able to go against the will of a town would be unthinkable. Madness. What is madness anymore, though? I see sigils in my dreams, calling to me, begging me to join them. They speak into my mind and tell me of secrets unspeakable and vague, tantalizing me with knowledge of forever. If that is not madness, then I shall never be mad. This all seems as if a fever dream now, my dear. Like a dream in which I walk unimpeded through a world that does not ascribe to the reason I once believed it operated by. A world where what I know to be true is nothing more than fantasy and that which I could never have dreamed in my worst nightmares is some sort of reality in which we work. This makes little sense. I feel my words slipping away from me. I shall drink another glass of peat wine to steady myself.

Ah, there we go! The world has returned to clarity, such as it is, for the moment. I may speak more of the festival. The town is ready to ring in a new era and they seem joyous. It is strange to see a feature other than moroseness on their faces, but there it is. It is unsettling in a way and I do not wish to continue considering why. Their joy is unholy, as is most of this town. God is not here, my darling. I wish He were, but something drove any sense of light away from this place long ago. God has been replaced by *[indecipherable]* and worse. ~~You must *[indecipherable]* before~~ -

February 13, 1922

My Luisa,

My love, how are you? It has been a fortnight
since I have heard from you and that grieves my
soul! I hope you are well. In town, the folk seem to
be gathering for some kind of festival. How unique!
It may be just what this place needs. It is always so
dreary and tiresome here that a festival of some
kind should be a nice respite, I must say. I may even
ask young Amleragh to attend with me - purely
platonically, my dove! She seems lonely and could
use a friend, as could we all. It has been a while
since I heard from that doctor up in Arkham. He has
not visited recently, and he never got back to me
about coming to visit. I find that quite rude indeed,
but you know how academics are! Heads buried in
their dusty tomes while the world goes by outside
them, eh what? I am sure we shall speak again, and
I would quite enjoy you coming along to explore
the university. You may even fall in love with the
town and want to relocate. Who knows? The future
is bright for us, my sweet Luisa. I am excited to see
what comes next.

Even in all the busyness around town, I still
ache for you. I miss you dearly and wish I could
come back to you. I have promised to find the
Weatherby boy, though, and must follow through
with my commitment to do just that. You know me,

love. Once I get my mind set on something, there is nothing in the world that can change it. That stubbornness comes from my father, you know. Did you ever meet him? I'm sure you must have, but I cannot remember a time when you did. My memory is a bit foggy, but that may be from the peat wine! Regardless, I have no doubt that he would love to meet you, as would my mother. ~~I believe they are still located in Philadelphia if you would like to drop by.~~

February 13, 1922

My Luisa,

My mother is dead. For five years now. What was I writing? Thinking? ~~It's like my hand writes what my brain wishes to be true~~, but that is foolish. I write what I like! ~~No, something compels me.~~ I write only the truth for you, my darling! The very depths of my heart and mind are bare for you as they have always been. I hide nothing from you and couch nothing so base as confusion in my text. Only words of love and longing for you, Luisa. That is what fills my mind, to the point that I wish to buy you a train ticket and bring you out here myself to join me here. As soon as we can manage, you shall join me!

[Editor's note: The following passage was written in indecipherable scribbles in a different language than English. I found later that it was an archaic form of Latin and managed to get it translated to the best of the ability available. It does not make complete sense, but I believe that its mere existence shines a light on more of where Boddicker's mental state was at this point in time. It is difficult to read.]

Water. I am in water. I am below water. Dark water. Deep water. Water filling my lungs. I breathe. I breathe and move like silk through the water. It is cold but soothing. No more heat from the sun. No more dryness. Water caressing me. Water pouring into me. It is peace. It is life. Water is life. Below the surface, it all aligns. I see something below. I dive effortlessly. I swim down to the bottom of the ocean with only a few strokes of my arms. I see fins. Webs. Normal. This is normal. This is right. Down to the bottom I go. I see the sigil in black stone. I see it scratched out, replaced by a face. Bulging eyes. Wide mouth. Fangs sharp and bared. This is who I am. This is who I believe I must be. This and only this. This

February 13, 1922

My Luisa,

Christ, what was that? What *was* that? Luisa, my love, I feel as if I am losing myself. Losing who I am. I do not know anymore. It is late at night. Early in the morning now, rather. Behind the clouds, I can see the moon staring at me, baleful in its gaze. Nothing near me is comfortable. Nothing around me is anything other than strange and frightening. Damn the Weatherbys! Damn them all. I must leave tomorrow. I *must*. I will walk back to the city if I must, but I cannot stay here another day. I cannot.

Wait for me, my love. I need you. I miss you.

Your Titus

February 14th, 1922

My lovely Luisa,

I am holed up in my room at the manor. I cannot imagine that you will ever receive this, but I must write it down, if only to prove to myself I have not gone wholly mad, though it feels that way. My darling, today was the festival. God help me. God help us all. I shall take a drink - a long drink - to steady the nerves and write all this down before it disappears from my mind. That shall be a mercy, but it must not be forgotten by the world. What remains of the world, perhaps. I know it sounds horrifying and hyperbolic, but my love, I mean every single word of it. One moment to breathe. One moment to feel air in my lungs.

Right. For posterity, then. I woke up in the morning to a day that appeared unlike any other in Innsmouth. Despite the omnipresent damp and grayness of the weather, there was a buzz about the city. A sense of life and urgency that bordered on frantic. I could feel it as soon as I stood up from my bed. There was an energy that ran deeper and darker than anything I had experienced, and I wanted nothing more than to scramble out the window and make my way the six miles down to the train station to simply get out of Innsmouth. However, I was cut short by a knock at the door. It was Harvey and he was practically glowing. He threw open my windows, revealing the same sick gray pallor that always existed, but remarked that it was a beautiful day. One of a million, he said. He told me that I should dress in my finest clothes and, in fact, he had taken the liberty to find me clothes that were suitable for the festival. He hoped I would take them and wear them as a token of our esteem and friendship and that ever-present sense of Catholic guilt tore at me. I could not refuse him. Not now. So, I dressed. It was a fine suit. Far finer than I had encountered in this town. Yet, when I put it on, it felt like I was wearing a costume or a uniform rather than something that would pass for high-class or gentility in a more civilized place. It was an outfit unsuited to the environment, but I wore it just the same. I must admit, my dear, that it felt quite nice to have something on that - for the moment - was not covered in wet or dry mud. I knew that would change, so I savored it while I could.

Breakfast was not a solemn affair as it often was. Harvey was chattering about this and that, excited about the festival. He told me about the events they had planned and how they were going to open the temple up to the community to see if they could drum up any more management. He talked at length about how out-of-towners would be joining us and hopefully many of them would stay to bolster the ranks of the town, especially since so many would be leaving. I chose not to ask why they would be leaving, as I could not come up with a response that would satisfactorily answer the question yet not horrify me to the core of my being. Still, it was nice to see him so upbeat for once. That energy was overshadowed, though, when Amleragh entered the room. She was dressed in a stunning ocean blue-green gown and had her hair primped as nicely as it could be. More than that, though, she was nearly glowing. There was a radiance and peace about her that I had only seen before in those women in town who had been with child. It did not register with me then. It does now. I want to vomit, my love, but there is nothing left inside me to purge. Only an empty pit where my sense of being once existed. But I speak too soon of that. In that moment, I only saw someone who was happy and that struck me in a way that brought my stomach to a churn. A place and a people so melancholy brought to joy is a concerning thing. Before I could argue that I was not feeling well, which was not a falsity as I felt quite ill, they ushered me out the door and we began walking to the shore. Amleragh looped her arm through mine possessively and added a small sashay to her step that would not have been out of place with a woman establishing possession over a partner. I believe that was precisely her intent.

The streets were packed with townsfolk and nearby farmers in droves thicker than I had ever conceived in this town. We brushed shoulders and bumped into person after person, yet there was no grumbling, no arguing, no sharp words. It was as if everyone had been driven into a stupor by the happiness of the day. It was the damnedest thing and, frankly, unsettling. We continued unabated, though, until we reached the temple. The crowd around the building was like a swarm of insects and Harvey, by virtue of being someone with power, ushered us through the mass of humanity (such as it was) and into the temple. He told me not to worry, that this was a day for celebration, and that all were welcome in the temple on this glorious occasion. He led us through the winding, twisting hallways - like intestines made of stone - until we reached a large banquet-style hall that I do not recall existing in my previous encounter with the temple, though much of that day remains vague and uncertain. Inside the hall, many chairs had been set up, including one heavy-looking stone throne up on a dais of a sort, though it had upon in a thick bluish pillow for the comfort of someone or something. Harvey led us to our seats, which were in the front row. This was not a mercy or a privilege, my love, as you shall see. He left us then, telling us to behave, and that he had to get dressed. That he was already dressed was irrelevant, as I suspected that he required a more ritual wardrobe. For the next several minutes, Amleragh talked at me aimlessly, saying more words than I had ever heard her speak before. I responded in short phrases, trying to appear uninterested, but I do not think it mattered what I said. She was beaming and, every so often, ran her hand over her stomach. I feared she had a kind of food poisoning. I was naive, my love.

Soon, though, the room was packed with villagers and dignitaries and the service began. Harvey stepped out in a queer-looking golden robe splashed with browns and blues, as well as wearing a golden mask. He announced himself to the group and the crowd roared in approval. He said that today was an historic day for Innsmouth and for the townspeople. That today we would see the return of the most beloved. That we had been blessed by the touch of the sea. That the love and partnership between the ocean and those present had been renewed and revivified. That today was a celebration of the joining of the two cultures that made Innsmouth the town it was. He urged us all to stand and welcome the peace offering, the vessel through which the relationship would be rebuilt.

It was at that point that two large men, dressed in suits but unmistakably fishy in their expressions, wheeled in young Lucien Weatherby. He was no longer as pallid as he had appeared before. No, my love, he was considerably, horrifically worse. His skin was pock-marked, shiny, and nigh-translucent. Even from where I sat, for I could not stand, I could see the blood in his veins. His face was sunken and dark and his eyes were dull. Nearly lifeless, honestly. His hair was sweaty and stuck to his face, as if he had been engaged in strenuous activity recently. More terrible than anything else, though, was the fact that his abdomen was swollen almost to the point of bursting. His stomach was distended and engorged, the skin stretching out like a balloon. He must have been in agony. Rather, he would have been had he not been poisoned by some kind of narcotic as evidenced by the angry red marks on the inside of his arms. As he was moved, a grotesque sloshing sound echoed, and I felt my heart seize as I realized the sound emanated from the bulging stomach of his. The wheelchair came to a halt and the two guards lifted him gently from his position and carried him to the throne, where he sat, moaning slightly through what must have been a significant haze.

Harvey cheered and bowed to Lucien as he was forcibly sat down. He announced to the throng around us, now filled with a low, primal growling, that the bearer of good news had arrived. I wonder if I should capitalize those words. It matters not, I suppose. He told us all that we were to be witnesses, glorious participants in the rebirth of their savior, Father Dagon. Through his sacrifice and pregnancy, Lucien had given himself over to be a vessel for their god. He was to be venerated as the new revival of Mother Hydra and would be properly honored once the ritual was complete. The time was almost nigh, Harvey announced with a rumble like a thousand storms, and the mood of the crowd turned from anticipatory to something close to feral. I looked for the exit, but it was behind me and blocked by several dozen chanting, howling, panting townsfolk. I was trapped, an unwilling prisoner, and could do nothing but sit and watch.

Lucien made a noise that turned my stomach and the chanting increased in earnest. The sound that came from that mouth was a mix of a wail, a sob, and a shriek of pain. The noise around me was heavy and intoxicating in the worst way. It dizzied me and the room seemed to fill with smoke. Harvey began chanting as well, adding his voice to the cacophony, as he reached over to a pulpit nearby. Had that always been here? I wasn't sure. Maybe it had. He retrieved a book - it was the same book as before - and began reading from it. Phrases and words poured out in languages never before heard by man. The townsfolk joined in, knowing the words by heart. I sat there, everything churning inside me, as I could do nothing but watch. Lucien's cries grew louder and clearer. The dull haze that had overtaken his gaze dissipated and, in that moment, I saw the true horror of his situation. He was not willing. He was not offering. He was being *made* a sacrifice and he began to scream as his stomach heaved and stretched. His keening cut through the wall of chanting and made every nerve in my spine quiver. There was no doubt in my mind now that his pain and terror was of a quality far beyond that which I could imagine.

As the sound reached a fever pitch, Harvey withdrew from the book something long and thin and shining golden. It was a blade, sharpened and polished to a gleam. He bellowed out something but closed with the words 'join us now, Father Dagon'. He then knelt before Lucien, pressed his forehead against the man's stomach in reverence, then took the knife and stabbed into the top of Lucien's stomach. The boy howled and a spurt of something thick and dark launched from the puncture wound to spatter on the townsfolk, all of whom roared in approval. With one swift motion, Harvey plunged the blade into the hole and drew it quickly downward. The knife split the skin of the boy's belly like it was tearing through tissue paper and a gush of heavy, gelid liquid (of a sort) poured from the incision and onto the floor. From where I was, I could only see that it was wriggling. I believe that the liquid contained nothing but small, black minnows. The smell was horrendous, like high tide on the beach, but the worst was yet to come. After the fluid had been released, Harvey reached inside the stomach cavity - Lucien had long since passed out, mercifully - and withdrew something the size of a breadbasket. It was somewhat cylindrical but had bumps and scales upon it. In front of it, two small hands, clawed and grasping, began to move. The cylinder shifted and moved and *opened its eyes*. Two orange-gold malevolent orbs peered out from what could only be the face and as this thing, this child, stretched its limbs out, I could see fangs already-yellowed in the maw of this creature. This was Father Dagon, reborn. Harvey held it aloft and the crowd, which seemed to stretch forever now, boomed and howled in a frenzy. I heard snapping jaws and frantic cries from desperate townsfolk, all aching to touch their god in the flesh. I had to leave. I needed to leave. I could not be there a moment longer. As the minnows thrashed and squirmed on the ground, as Lucien bled and gurgled something unintelligible, as the townsfolk fell to chaos, as Harvey lifted to the sky the reincarnation of a literal god, all I could do was scream along with the crowd and close my eyes. I wanted to be somewhere else. I had to be. I could feel the limits of my mind straining with the stress of what I was experiencing, and it felt like Hell on Earth. My love, I did not know if I would make it out of there alive, especially when Harvey sat the child down on the pulpit. It yawned and blinked and the crowd stared, enraptured.

By now, Lucien's gurgling had stopped, and he was truly dead. I cannot imagine what his final moments were like, but I hope that Heaven and our Lord God treat him to a penthouse suite for all the suffering he endured in the end. Harvey grasped the wrist of the dead boy and dragged the body to the edge of the dais. He cried out happily that Mother Hydra had accomplished her task and had left us. Now it was time to honor her as she deserved. With that, he heaved the corpse of Lucien Weatherby into the crowd and they began to eat. Ripping, tearing, chewing, smacking, crunching, cracking. The sounds were hideous, nearly worse than those that came from the boy earlier, and I felt everything around me turn into a blur of dizziness. I passed out there, my darling, and I did not know if I would ever return.

I came to in my room in the manor. A cold compress was on my forehead and Amleragh was sitting next to me, a concerned look on her pretty face. She did not have the glow from before. Instead, she appeared worried about me. How strange to think that this person - if she were a person - would bother herself with me when her god had resurrected itself from the ashes. When she saw I was awake, she smiled and caressed my hand. I asked her what had happened, as I was unsure of myself. She told me that I became overwhelmed at the temple with the heat and bodies around and fainted. As soon as I fell, I had been whisked away and brought back to the manor to recuperate. She said that there was no shame in having lost my senses, as oftentimes such events reach a fever pitch that is too much for some, especially outsiders. She assured me that nobody was judging me and that many were impressed that I had lasted so long as I did in the environment. I did not dare tell her that I had been physically incapable of leaving the room. Better for others to think me brave than a trapped coward, yes? It was certainly a balm for my bruised ego.

Amleragh told me to rest and, when I tried to stand, placed a hand on my chest to stop me. She said that I needed time to recover fully, and that calmness would be the best thing for me. Was there anything I needed? Water? Food? I told her that I was alright and that I was feeling fine. At that point, she laid down next to me and rested her head on my chest. I must admit, my love, that it was comforting to have the presence of someone next to me. It has been so long since I have been with you, seen you, held you, kissed you. My fault as well as yours, of course! But having her nestled up against me felt quite nice. It was innocent and intimate at the same time. She whispered in my ear that she wanted me to stay with her for a while. I did not need to sleep but having me there with her was what she wanted. I could not turn her down. I...I did not want to do so.

Luisa, my dove, my heart has grown heavy with conflict. I wish to return to you, but she is here. No matter, I suppose. I needs must leave at my earliest opportunity. I am here alone now, as Amleragh has left to join the festivities, and I have been swimming within my thoughts. I relaxed and calmed as we lay there, but as I recall the events of the temple, I am returned to my anxiety and discomfort. I know that what I saw was not a figment of my imagination. I know that somewhere in this town, a small child, a baby god, resides. It sleeps and eats and grows bit by bit. And I can do nothing about it but sit and wait for the future to come.

No. No, my love. That cannot be. Will not be. No, I must find a solution to my thoughts and dreams and future, whatever the cost. I must or I shall drown.

Continue your prayers for me, my sweet. I shall need them in the days to come.

Yours always,

Titus

February 19th, 1922

My Luisa,

It is the middle of the night as I write this. The stars are out and the moon glares down at me with a baleful glow. I tried to sleep. I tried. I managed to do so for a while. But then they came to me. The dreams. They do not leave me alone. They follow me wherever I go. I am haunted by them. So, now, I sit and write until the sun comes up and I may begin my day. The dreams...Luisa, I do not know how much more I can bear of them.

I can no longer be sure that I am not in actual danger. What worries me the most is that the shadow figure in my dream has been speaking to me, especially within the dream. He has whispered secrets into my head that I cannot express in any human words. He has told me of a world, a universe really, far outside the realm that is comprehensible to myself or any man or woman alive or dead. He speaks of a mighty writhing mass of tentacles and eyes, all slumbering peacefully as horns and flutes and drums echo in a cacophony of madness around the creature. These sounds, this music, it keeps this thing asleep for, if it wakes, all that is, was, and will be shall become forfeit. It shall disappear as we are naught but the manifestations of its dreaming. It is ridiculous, of course. The idea that we are nothing but dreams is patently false, lies from a hidden trickster. Still, I cannot help but wonder if there is nothing true about what he has told me or if there is something, some kernel of veracity, which lurks in the corners of his words. Are we not alone? Are we helpless? I cannot know, my love, but the thought that you and I are figments of some cosmic monster and nothing more is...hideous. Unthinkable. I cannot bear it.

So, my love, I sit here in my room with only a candle to keep me company. I am weary but I cannot sleep. If I sleep, I may not wake again. It sounds foolish, I know. Something tells me otherwise, however. I shall simply stay here until the sun rises.

~~lord nyarlathotep free me from this plane free me from the pain of existence take me in your dark arms and guide me to the perpetual chaos that is the outer realm~~

February 19th, 1922

My Luisa,

I have just woken up again, my darling. I slept fitfully. Apparently, I wrote something down but have scratched it out with great vigor. I cannot let you see the madness that has poured out of me. I must walk around. I must get food. Perhaps the more I can unearth about what happened at the temple, the closer I will get to figuring out what has happened to me and to my life. Where I went wrong. I have seen my dreams and they have consumed me, but it may not be too late. I hope not. I can only hope that we shall be reunited soon. That is all that drives me. That is all that keeps me going. I have not succumbed to despair yet, angel, because of you. Because of what you mean to my life.

Soon, I will unchain what has been tormenting my mind and I shall release it into the aether where it may dissipate and die like so many summer breezes - hot, reeking of animal fat maybe. Such a grotesque image and that is not how I have experienced summers, except with your pigs of relatives. What do I *write*? My dove, please forgive the cruelty with which I peppered this last bit of writing. It is not my heart, but you know this. You know who I am and what I feel for you and those close to you. I value all of them as I value you. My mind and body are tired. That is the best explanation I can provide for you at this time. It is not that I truly feel those things deep inside. It is not that I am agonized over the thought of losing you to those demons in town. It is not that I believe you to be mine and will fight tooth and claw to exterminate any and all who attempt to steal you away from me. ~~I shall fight them until the cobblestones run red with their hot, steaming blood. Until the fumes of their lives waft into the air and choke the clouds with their foul odor. Until their brains are bashed into a fine paste and ground into dirt. Until they are cut open and their entrails scattered about as if fat snakes wanting to escape the toxicity that pollutes their innards. God, I hate them. I hate all of them. I wish them all to be torn asunder and I can make that happen. I shall! I shall turn them into pies for the needy and fodder for the cattle to sup upon in their darkest hours. They shall feed the fields with their bodies and their souls shall exit and belong to whomever wishes to claim them. Yes, Luisa. Yes, my love. I shall do all this for love of you. Only then, when all your suiters have been turned to mulch and bone, shall I be able to rest. Truly rest. Yes, I see it now. I see that I have been too passive. Too genteel~~.

What was that? What on God's green earth was any of that? My love, I swear to you with everything inside of me that I do not wish harm to anyone! Certainly not to those whom you call your friends. The idea that I could cause such vicious

169

violence to anyone is beyond the pale. I am not that kind of man, my darling, and I know that you know that. Much more of this and I could write more horrible lies and brutality that work within me without me knowing so. I do not know when I shall be able to write again, my Luisa. I hope soon. I truly do. Perhaps fresh air will give me a moment of peace.

Your loving Titus

February 20th, 1922

My darling Luisa,

The air did not help. I wandered and slogged my way through the muck and mud once more. The townsfolk went about their business. Ignored me. I was invisible. I am invisible. They do not see me or choose not to. I wandered around and found myself at the temple. A wave of nausea struck my stomach and I braced myself against the sandstone.

I went mad then, I think, and closed my eyes. When I opened them once more, I was not in the room. I did not know where I was until I looked up and saw a sun shrouded in darkness. It felt as if I were in a dream, but this was real. It was *real*, my love. As real as you or me. I bent down and felt the ground. Sand. Soft and hot. I picked up a handful and lifted it to my face. It was strange. Maroon, no, blood-red, no, something in-between. A constantly shifting form of red, to be sure. When I opened my hand, the grains spilled out in a torrent to rejoin their compatriots and it was as if I had opened a vein and allowed the claret to stream out of me. It was only sand, though. It had to be. I breathed in and could not discern a particular scent to the air. Something spiced mutely. Rot and decay. Sticky-sweet. It was all smells and none at once. The intensity of it all drove me to my knees and I felt despair wash over me like the roiling sea. I was

Jonah, being swallowed by a beast far larger than I could comprehend. I was being punished. I was without hope.

It was then that he came to me. He knelt down in front of me and lifted my chin with his hand. It was colder than ice and scaled, with long, sharp nails, but the simple touch was comfort incarnate. His face was *[Editor's note: These were not words. They were simply letters and smears of something dark and long-since dried.]*

He was terrible and beautiful and pulses of black power streamed from his many eyes. He called himself *Nyarlathotep.* A name that stuck in my heart like a blade and has not left. With incomprehensible growls and laughs, he told me that he saw great potential in me. He said that he had felt the presence of another of his kind being brought into the world. He spoke of Father Dagon and the cosmic balance being upset. Of ancient pacts being breached and greed and envy bleeding into our world. He said things I could not understand, but I did grasp what he wanted. He desired what I desired - the end of Dagon. He assured me with forked tongues that he did not wish to become corporeal. He too much enjoyed wandering the dreams of the unwary and careless and curious. He found too much pleasure in pulling strings like a marionette. My stomach grew sick upon hearing his glee at the wars and conflicts scourging the world, but he told me - instructed me, perhaps - to look beyond my morality, my ethics, my soul, my sense of right and wrong. He took my hand in his and lifted me to my feet and we were in a city. One older than time, ruins crumbled and rebuilt and destroyed and turned to dust over and over in an endless cycle of destruction and rebirth. It brought a tear to my eye, though I could not tell you if it was due to beauty or terror. Perhaps both, my love. Perhaps both.

This creature, this *Nyarlathotep* - I shall not use his name again for fear of calling upon him - brought a charm and calm to the situation as we walked. He talked about this place, this lost Carcosa, and the king in tatters that ruled over it. I looked around and Ny- the creature laughed, a sonorous echo from deep within the bowels of the earth. He told me that this king, to be and remain unnamed for the safety of all, was toothless when unacknowledged. It could not strike at those who did not speak its name and so it was forced to sit on its throne and reach into the dreams of the weary, probing a finger into their thoughts and planted its name like a poisonous seed within the unconscious mind of the victim or servant.

This dark being told me in no uncertain terms that I had nothing to fear from the King in Yellow. He would protect me from the tyrant. He would protect me from all dangers, both of this reality and ours. He would bring me riches and my heart's desire. He would grant me power beyond measure, the seat of nations from which I could enact his will. I would be his avatar, his voice. All I needed to do was swear my fealty and undertake the task of exterminating the infant Father Dagon. When I did so, he said, I would become more than anyone had ever been before. I would be a legend and my name carved into the sunken stars of R'lyeh and the outer limits of the multiple realities. He said that nothing would be beyond my grasp. Nothing, of course, save control of him or of his master. All else that existed, including his friends, enemies, allies, and acquaintances, would fall under his banner as I waved it to signal his victory. He would not overtake me, he promised. He would not break a debt. He would do as he promised. What reason would he have to do otherwise?

I wanted to believe him, Luisa. I did. I really, truly did. I wanted his words to be true. Such power! Such esteem! Such fame! All that I have been missing in my life would be in my hands for the first time. I would have you, by my side, dressed in the finest clothes. You would be a woman of such dignity and respect that nobody would dare to raise a word to you, both out of deference to you and due to fear of me and what I could do.

My Luisa, if he were telling the truth, the improvement in my life and your life would have been immeasurable. I hoped beyond all reason for proof to believe. My love, I could not find any. As tempting as all of it was, as much as my heart's desires were there, sitting in front of me, simply waiting to be plucked as if ripe fruit from a drooping tree limb, I found myself returning to one thought: this was not what you would have wanted for me. You knew me to be no fool. You still do. Why then would I take a fool's bargain? Even *if* this creature spoke true, what of my immortal soul? What is left of it, rather, but you understand my meaning. What bargain would I be striking? What would I be sacrificing to achieve my dreams?

He sensed my reluctance, I could tell. He laughed and the sound was a snake shivering on velvet sheets. It scraped across my ears and poured into my skull. He knew the human thoughts I was having. Of course he did. He understood them and did not begrudge me them. He would not force me to do a thing but asked only that I permit him to tell me one thing more in order to convince me. I believed I could give him that much so I agreed. He slithered over to me and placed his long, scaled hand on my shoulder. He leaned in close and I closed my eyes so as not to see his horrible visage. I smelt the grave and death and rot and something sweet and sickly. It was a horrendous odor. I felt my bones quiver inside me, but I could not move. In my ear, he whispered a secret I cannot express in words. It cut deep into my being and something changed. In that moment, I became someone other than myself.

Luisa, I accepted his offer.

I love you.

Your beloved Titus

February 24th, 1922

My Luisa,

I returned to Harvey on bended knee and apologized for my rudeness as of late. My absence. My distance. I told him he deserved more of a guest, but he would hear none of it. He embraced me as a brother and called for Amleragh to make my room spotless. She appeared around the corner and, though I cannot be sure, I believe that she was more well-rounded than before, so to speak. She appeared delighted to see me and led me upstairs to where I once had slept and dreamt the dreams of the mostly righteous. She told me how happy she was that I was here and that we would need to speak in the coming days about what the future held. I did not think much of it at the time. I know differently now, but I get ahead of myself.

I hope you are well, my dear. It seems like an age and a half since I have seen you, held you, kissed your brow. Time has lost meaning anymore and I can do nothing but sit back and be swept along with the tide. I am certain you feel the same way and can only imagine how much you ache for my return. It shall come soon. I have one task to perform and then I shall be back with you and will enter a new world where we are above all. I can scarcely believe how soon it shall be! I need only complete the singular duty put to me and then I am free.

My love, I must kill the child Dagon.

It sounds much worse than it is, you know. I am not committing murder. Certainly not murder on a child. That monstrosity is no child, nothing so full of innocence as that. No, Luisa, that *thing* is an abomination. It should not be and soon it shall not be.

I will keep this letter brief, my darling. I have planning to do. When next you hear from me, I hope to whatever gods can hear me that it will be with joyous news and triumph.

I am still yours.

Your Titus.

February 25th, 1922

My darling,

I am currently barricaded inside my room at Harvey's manor, and he is banging on the door, demanding answers and justice.

I have little time so I cannot spare much for pleasantries. Only a record of what I have done will be acceptable.

The child is - was - being cared for by several townsfolk at the temple. A steady rotation of visitors and well-wishers came in, would offer small treats or gifts to the child, and leave with the gurgled assumption of a blessing from their savior. I asked the few townsfolk in front of the entrance if I would be allowed to provide a gift to the infant Dagon and, though my question was met with understandable skepticism, I explained that I had been front and center at the god's birth and was overwhelmed with ecstasy at its presence. It was not entirely a falsity on my part, though the word 'ecstasy' was a bit much. Whatever the case, such a claim seemed to appease the guards and they stepped aside to allow me entrance. They did not search me. They did not find the cold, wrought-iron dagger tucked into my belt. The dagger that, upon waking this morning, was sitting on my desk with thin wisps of dark smoke emanating from it. The dagger that felt like a heartbeat pulsing against my body.

Walking through the temple felt as if I were swimming through a thick layer of murky water. My body did not feel like my own. Perhaps it was not. I took my place at the back of the hall where the throng waited anxiously for their turn to be blessed. In a minute or two, a bassinet was wheeled out by the priests. The child Dagon was couched inside. Even though I could not see the entirety of the creature, I saw scaly hands grasping at the sky. With remarkable cooperation, those in the hall formed into a queue to wait. I made sure to be as near the back of the line as possible, as I wanted to be able to escape as soon as I had done my dirty business. Slowly, achingly so, the line ticked by one by one until it was my turn. As the townsperson in front of me finished up what they said, I was waved up to the dais and told to present my gift to the new god. I nodded and stepped past the priests to see the beast.

Had I not known what it was, I would dare to say I would have called it 'cute' in some abhorrent way. The form of it was reminiscent of a child, but the details were wrong. The color, the shape, the claws and teeth...all of it was unmistakably fishy. As it lay there, it opened its eyes and the burning orange in its eyes cut for just a moment through the darkness around my heart. It saw what I came to do.

It *knew*. It could not stop me. No, it *would* not stop me. Those eyes, they told me that I was taking my future in my hands and taking the future of the world away from those that deserved it. Immense guilt and shame washed over me, and I nearly stepped back, but my hand reached into my belt and withdrew the dagger. The metal felt hot in my hand and, before I could do anything to stop it, the knife came down and plunged into the chest of the child monster. A burst of dark, icy ichor launched from the wound as the creature screeched and then died and then I was running running running shoving my way through the stunned crowd they began to scream and roar in fury and tried to stop me but I lashed out with the dagger over and over and over and blood sprayed and people fell back and the door was there and I ran through it and bells rang and people howled and I ran up the road with blood trailing from the blade of the dagger and I smashed into the door of the manor and made it up the stairs and into my room and I put up a barricade and now I am here and oh God what have I done I have killed a child no not a child a demon I did something good something good something heroic yes something heroic -

The bangs on the door are getting louder, my love. The wood is not splintering yet, but it shall soon. I hope you get this. I hope you know how much I love you and how much you mean to me. I want to be with you, Luisa. It may take longer than I expect.

Your loving Titus

February 26th, 1922

Luisa,

I escaped. Somehow. It does not matter. None of it does.

I am no longer myself. I am someone other than. I have given myself over to the dark one. He is here. He is me.

He lied.

No longer your Titus

February 29th, 1922

Beautiful one, you should visit. Come join me. Join us. You shall see wonders beyond what you can imagine. Come. Be with me. You shall be loved.

Titus

March 45th, 1922222222

Luisa,

I am lost.

Titus

From the desk of the Editor:

Reader, that was the last message that Luisa Treadwell received from Titus Boddicker. After she sent them to me, she sent another missive informing me that she was concerned that those who read these letters may get the wrong impression of her relationship with Mr. Boddicker. The letter follows thusly:

Dear Mr. Trench,

I thank you deeply for taking this burden from my shoulders. It has weighed heavy on my heart, and I wish to be part of it no further. I do, however, feel some concern that the contents of the letters from Mr. Boddicker may imply a relationship that he and I unequivocally did not have. If you will permit me to correct the narrative, I would be most appreciative.

I shall say this as plainly and frankly as possible. Mr. Titus Boddicker and I were never in a relationship. Not once. He became enamored with me upon visiting my house in his role as a solicitor and became obsessive and discomfiting with his exuberance and fascination with me. I have been happily married to Linus Treadwell for several years now and I intend to remain as such until the day I die. Mr. Boddicker would not - could not - accept this fact and, as such, developed an alternate reality for himself in which he and I were betrothed, and my husband was some sort of interloper in a divine relationship. That is and was patently false and I shall accept no such claims to the contrary.

I did not burn these letters because I believed, for a time, that I should have to utilize their contents in a civil trial to get him to abstain from contacting either my family or myself. However, as the letters became more troubling, I must admit that I found them to be fascinating in a morbid sort of way. Clearly, Mr. Boddicker was dealing with something that he was unable to cope with himself and I pity him all the more for it.

I believe Mr. Boddicker suffers - or suffered - from a significant mental impairment for which he should have received clinical aid. I mourn the loss of every human being, but those who are afflicted with troubles of the mind are particularly heartbreaking. Though I do not owe him a thing, I should like to announce henceforth that my husband and I will be funding a charity to provide help to those most in need of freedom from their own thoughts. It is the least we can do. All profits, few as they are likely to be, from this book you compile shall be given to said charity so that Mr. Boddicker may finally have the recognition he wished for in life.

I appreciate what you are doing for myself and my family, Mr. Trench. This nightmare of a troubled man shall hopefully soon pass us by. Perhaps this record of the descent of an innocent, if obnoxious, man into a self-inflicted torturous madness shall provide new life to the field of psychiatry.

God bless you and keep you safe, sir.

Mrs. Luisa Treadwell

So, you see, dear readers, that the letters that Mr. Boddicker sent to someone he thought his beloved were nothing more than fantasies created by an ill mind. It is a pity, no doubt, that such a man could suffer so without others helping him. I hope only that he has found peace at last.

Solomon Trench

Editor-in-Chief, Poughkeepsie Tribune

From the desk of the Editor:

One final note, dear readers. Though this book heads shortly to print, I find that the letter I received just this morning is too important, for lack of a better word, to leave out from the text. I am unhappy to understand that reality, mind you. Though it says little and, on the surface, seems to be a standard announcement, knowing what I know, it disturbs me to my core, my friends. Once the letter has been transcribed here, which shall not be long in doing, it shall be put to the hottest flame I am able to find. I no longer wish to see my friend alive. I no longer hope for his survival. Instead, I am deeply aggrieved that this missive has shown the contrary. I was foolish to hope for better and am sorry and ashamed of my naivete. I shall no more be a part of these proceedings. The book shall be sent to market as a cautionary tale, and I shall retreat to somewhere I cannot be found. I apologize, dear readers, but this is the end of my tale. I wash my hands of this. Do not try to contact me.

Solomon Trench

Former Editor-in-Chief, Poughkeepsie Tribune

To Mr. Solomon Trench,

Mr. and Mrs. Titus and Amleragh Boddicker are delighted to inform you of the birth of their child Darren Goncalo Boddicker at the time of 9:33 on August 22, 1922. The child weighed 4 pounds, 7 ounces and was 33 inches long. Both mother and child are happy, healthy, and settling in at home.

In lieu of gifts, the Boddickers would like to extend to you a personal invitation to a gathering and celebration at the home of the proud grandfather, Mr. Harvey Marsh, this Saturday the 29th of August. There shall be cake and champagne, so please dress in your finest. Your presence as a family friend is requested and would be a delight to the entire Boddicker clan.

Hail Father Dagon

Mayor Harvey Marsh

About The Author

A.C. Cross is a doctor, but not the kind that you want treating you for kidney stones or pneumonia or anything. That'd likely make your situation much worse.

He (currently) lives in the Great White North of the United States as a bearded, somewhat-handsome man, depending on who you ask.

He's a lover of words, many of which you have just read in this very book.

He's an admitted scotch whisky and beer snob and his liver would not argue with him.

He is the author of the Roboverse series of books as well as *Where Blood Runs Gold* and *Zoo.*

You can find more about him as well as some neat little free stories at www.aaronccross.com.